HOW I WON
A NOBEL PRIZE

HOW I WON A NOBEL PRIZE

A Novel

JULIUS TARANTO

Little, Brown and Company

New York Boston London

Copyright © 2023 by Julius Taranto

Hachette Book Group supports the right to free expression and the value of copyright. The purpose of copyright is to encourage writers and artists to produce the creative works that enrich our culture.

The scanning, uploading, and distribution of this book without permission is a theft of the author's intellectual property. If you would like permission to use material from the book (other than for review purposes), please contact permissions@hbgusa.com. Thank you for your support of the author's rights.

Little, Brown and Company
Hachette Book Group
1290 Avenue of the Americas, New York, NY 10104
littlebrown.com

First Edition: September 2023

Little, Brown and Company is a division of Hachette Book Group, Inc. The Little, Brown name and logo are trademarks of Hachette Book Group, Inc.

The publisher is not responsible for websites (or their content) that are not owned by the publisher.

The Hachette Speakers Bureau provides a wide range of authors for speaking events. To find out more, go to hachettespeakersbureau.com or call (866) 376-6591.

Interior book design by Marie Mundaca

ISBN 978-0-316-51307-4

LCCN is available at the Library of Congress

Printing 1, 2023

LSC-C

Printed in the United States of America

To Allison, of course

HOW I WON
A NOBEL PRIZE

1.

The Rubin Institute had nothing to do with high-temperature superconductors, so I cannot say I had spent much time thinking about it.

Hew explained the whole drama: We thought we had purged our moral grotesques—the harassers, racists, bigots, zealots. The problem was these people technically had contracts. They held equity, tenure, real estate. They were hanging around the universities we thought we had shooed them from. Important conferences on graph theory and seventeenth-century Welsh agriculture were being derailed by disconcerted whispers that *he* had showed up and had the *temerity* to ask a question of the panel.

So there was some appeal to the idea that these people would now go live on an island in the North Atlantic. This new Institute said: Give me your cancellees and deplorables, your preeminent deviants, we'll take them! The popular vision, at the beginning, was of an academic prison colony where the worst-behaved of great minds would live out their days, closed off from the pleasures of civilized life.

We had not, Hew said, expected them to have such a good time. We had not expected the footage of one probable bigot and one confirmed groper strolling across lush seaside lawns, sitting on a slim white beach, clinking their Fields Medals in a taunting toast, it seemed, to every despicable act they had never paid for. It turned out the last thing these people wanted was *our* civilization. At the Rubin Institute Plymouth they had their own. It was a libertarian, libertine dream: bottomless funding, unencumbered by institutional regulations. They screwed students and eschewed trigger warnings. The enticing promise the Institute made to faculty was: No Code of Conduct, no Human Resources, only Your Work. The promise it made to students—wait, there would be students??—this promise was: Learn from geniuses, graduate *sans* debt, feel free to carry mace.

The Institute was shooting the moon, taking the human discards that no one else wanted, and winning. The place became a media fixation. Its faculty were enemies of the people—we had wanted them exiled—but then they had not been sent to Siberia! It was Sandals for scandals, with tax-exempt status.

The prior year 122 Presidential Merit Scholars had passed up Harvard to go there for free. It was an outrage. It could not go on.

Demonstrations ran perpetually on the New Haven pier. This was where the ferry departed for Plymouth Island, which the Institute had purchased entire. The pier was ground zero for all the wrong the Institute represented. It was a nuclear testing site, an oil pipeline on Indigenous land; now and then someone chained herself across the gangplank.

Hew and I watched the ferry's burbling stern nudge into the dock.

Meanwhile thirty or forty protesters, probably Yale undergraduates, waved signs along the lines of Benefit Is Complicity; Attendance Is Assent.

Hew clutched my hand. He smirked apologetically at no one in particular. This was an attempt to communicate that the situation was not how it appeared. It was not him, not the tall blondish man, but rather the small Jewish woman beside him who had compelled us to move to what several nearby signs called Rape Island.

2.

The reason did have something to do with high-temperature superconductors.

Ordinarily when we move electricity, through wires and circuits and batteries, we lose a lot of it along the way, as heat. Conductors are leaky pipes, but they're all we have. Hence laptops and phones get hot; faulty wires cause fires.

But some materials can transfer nearly unlimited energy over nearly unlimited distances with nearly no leakage, no loss. Superconductors. Electrons move through them unobstructed, swiftly. Superconductors are like those pneumatic tubes in old department stores.

Think of the potential! Move energy *freely,* without losing heat in transit, and you could have a sustainable global power grid in about ten years. You could have server farms without billions per annum in air conditioning. You could have safe fusion power, cost-effective seawater desalination, MRI machines as ubiquitous as smartwatches.

Over time these things would save a few billion lives. They'd save the planet.

Many materials, e.g., aluminum or zinc, can superconduct at temperatures near absolute zero. Some less-common materials can do it at higher temperatures that are still very cold. The problem is we do not know why. Nor do we know how to make any materials superconduct at anywhere near the temperatures and pressures found on Earth. We do not understand the fundamental principles involved, the key elements. All we know is that the right materials must be placed under the right conditions. The conditions under which they thrive must be understood, then created, for the potential of these strange materials to be realized.

Conditions that are amenable to high-temperature superconductors might be hostile to everyday aluminum. Conversely, a high-temp superconductor might be perfectly useless, highly resistant, under conditions where aluminum conducts itself with aplomb.

The special condition under which I thrived was collaboration with Perry Smoot.

Thus we had to go to RIP.

3.

My subject was the Zhou-Eisenstadt-Smoot Theoretical Model. After college I had declined lucrative offers from Google and J.P. Morgan so that I might toil in graduate studies under the supervision of Smoot himself. Newton and Leibniz concurrently invented calculus; Smoot, concurrently and eventually in collaboration with Zhou and Eisenstadt, modeled the relation between pressure and superconductivity. Their theory's predictions bore out, plotting the curve of experimentally measured electrical resistance almost exactly. ZEST was accurate to so many decimal places that Zhou, Eisenstadt, and Smoot were asked to meet the King of Sweden.

Still, the whole superconductivity phenomenon was barely understood. The ZEST model was the best that had been done, but it was hardly a comprehensive account. I was unusually promising. I had been told I might have the capacity to improve ZEST, even to render it general— the kind of thing that would mean a Nobel of my own.

At the very least I could contribute to the field. Provided the right advisor would guide me. Zhou was in China. Eisenstadt: dead in a dreadful accelerator accident, particles everywhere. Perry Smoot and Cornell University: eager to take me on. He said we had the same kind of mind, which in retrospect should have concerned me.

I should have known something was amiss when Perry was in his office on a Friday. This had never happened in over four years. Then one Friday he was at his desk, on the phone, a nod to me as I passed on my way to lab. Curious! I thought. But there was code to write, test, rewrite. At this point Perry did not trust anyone besides me to write his code. Our model was an attempt to simulate the flow of electricity through candidate high-temp superconductors. We passed the model back and forth like a relay baton, and I felt we were making progress almost daily; I was alive with it. So I was not thinking about how it must have taken something dire for Perry to be on campus on Friday. I was not thinking that the target of an internal investigation does not generally select the date of his administrative hearing.

When he was again in his office on *Saturday,* I should have thought: This is a five-alarm fire. Instead I was thinking that there was obviously a better way to sum interlayer Josephson interactions, but could it be done without iterating the Markov-chain quantum Monte Carlo algorithm (which would of course create *insurmountable* computing problems)?

The following Wednesday, Perry was again in his office and I was beckoned to enter.

Perry appeared as usual. He tilted back in his immense executive desk chair, draped in a seersucker sports coat, miles of starched fabric spanning his huge stomach, fingers clasped across a wide tie speckled with tiny equestrians. He was a big brilliant queer of the Oxbridge style. He had clean round jowls and wide round eyes beneath a clean wide round bald head. A geologically bald head.

Perry said, You and I will be moving to the Rubin Institute.

Why? I said.

Devlin, he said.

Really.

Devlin was one of my peers, nominally. But his code was clunky and inefficient, his models sadly lacking in physical intuition. Whether he completed his degree or not, Devlin was destined to thrive at J.P. Morgan.

Perry said, The rule these days, apparently, is that Nobel Prize winners may fuck *only* other Nobel Prize winners. Perry's insistent round eyes waited for me to laugh.

I don't want to go to the Rubin Institute, I said.

I was not as intensely Online as Hew, did not yet know all of the historical particulars, but I knew generally why one went to the Rubin Institute and who one's company there would be.

Perry said, Do you intend to learn Mandarin?

Hew will not want to go to the Rubin Institute, I said.

Unless you intend to work with Zhou, there *is no one* for you besides me, and I am going to the Rubin Institute. It is all arranged. We have funding. Your credits will transfer.

I massaged my temples with my fingers.
We need each other, Helen.
How could you have—?
It is for the best, said Perry, imperturbable.
It won't be your ass getting pinched.
Oh please.
I stood and said: Zai jian.

4.

Hew had sufficient outrage for the both of us. So reckless! Even setting aside Devlin—poor Devlin!— doesn't Perry see how it hurts others? Affects us! We hitched our wagon!

I thought: Yes, and what about disrupting delicate daily progress on high-temperature superconductivity??

Perry had almost unprecedented ability to diagonalize a matrix but was as dumb as anyone, apparently, when it came to sex. Probably he did not have much of it. Devlin on the other hand was handsome and he knew it. He was confident, toned, sensual. We had known each other pretty well at the beginning of grad school, but within a couple of years we'd diverged onto different tracks. Devlin skipped conferences to hang out in the city. I could not say it aloud, even to Hew, but I thought if I had to place bets on who started it, who was really in control...

So it was hard to be mad about the sex. What I was mad about was that according to Devlin, according to the

Times, Perry had said he would recommend Devlin to Caltech. Such a recommendation was a career guarantee. You could accomplish nothing for the rest of your life and still you would be considered brilliant, promising, someone whom Perry Smoot had recommended to Caltech. Meanwhile Devlin was not even allowed to *touch* Perry's code! Perhaps Devlin had discerned that Perry would not, could not, really follow through vis-à-vis Caltech? Anyway there was hard evidence, emails, texts. Devlin showed these to the university's Title IX Coordinator. The hearing was a formality. Perry admitted responsibility.

Shortly thereafter—perhaps the same day?—Perry made arrangements with the Rubin Institute. Nobel laureate, canceled for a noncriminal infraction, working on high-temp superconductors. Fellows like Perry were RIP's very *raison.* They said, When can you get here?

Anyway Hew persuaded me that we could absolutely *not* go to the Rubin Institute.

For a semester we tried not going to the Rubin Institute.

But only one man is the S in ZEST. There is one Large Hadron Collider; the rest of physics is human capital. Perry was unique. Without him the model stalled. I was writing code that might be mistaken for Devlin's— mired in bugs and bad assumptions that Perry would have seen around. Our simulation seemed suddenly far too big for me to attempt alone. I could not demonstrate even incremental progress when no one besides Perry and myself, and sometimes not even us, had any clue what the end state might look like. The department tried to step in, to help Perry's orphans. But no one else had been so tightly linked to him. I was helpless even to articulate the problems I was up against.

Ithaca is a particularly dreary place to lack purpose. I wrote pleading 2 a.m. emails to Zhou using automated translation. When these proved indecipherable, I audited Mandarin 101 for a few months and finally lost Zhou altogether after pasting 1200 lines of code into an email. Subject: PLEASE QING BANG WO!!

July, I called Perry.

August, I told Hew I had called Perry.

Hew admitted that he had never seen me so miserable. Yet the Rubin Institute, Cancel U—just impossible! Hew asked: Really, how hard is Mandarin? Really, would it be the *worst* to work at J.P. Morgan?

I said, You are a socialist.

Better than RIP.

So would I have to go alone?

Now he understood the gravity of the situation.

5.

It was a matter of some uncertainty whether Hew and I were married.

Well, we unquestionably were married, from a legal standpoint, as we had at one point early on required a marriage license to share subsidized graduate housing. At issue was whether we had ever transformed this technicality into a proper marriage through simultaneous shared intention, a meeting of the minds, a synchronized mutual commitment.

At one point I had been sure we really were married, but then Hew said something like, When we get married properly... So then I was sure we were not. Then a few months later I might say, in passing, When we get married properly... and Hew would look up and ask: Do you think we're not married yet?? The condition was unstable, evading description. It was Schrödinger's wedlock; we were both hitched and not.

Soon it became a game. One of us might assert, for instance: We will be spending the rest of our lives together, so we really should be in agreement about X. The other was then obliged to say: We will? Or, another instance, Hew might introduce me to a new acquaintance as: My spouse, Helen. To which I would say: I am??

Any failure from Partner B to deny the marriage asserted by Partner A would, it was understood, result in the end of the game: matrimony.

So I now said to Hew: I can't believe you would want me to go to the Rubin Institute alone. You're my husband.

Am I?

A school of chauvinists, harassers, genuine rapists, Hew—not to mention racists, anti-Semites. You are saying I should go there, to this *island,* nowhere to run, *without my spouse.*

I am *saying,* said Hew, that you should not go at all. You can do without Perry. I believe in you. Also, who's your spouse?

I don't know.

You don't know that I believe in you?

I don't know that I can do it without Perry—or that he can do it without me. I doubt anyone could build this model alone. Probably we need a whole firm of engineers, an Army corps.

Except for how you don't trust other people.

A clone army then. Myself multiplied tenfold and Perry multiplied...maybe twice?

If cloning Perry were required to save the world, it might not be worth it.

I said: You think you're joking, but that actually gets to the heart of it. I don't understand why you get so caught up in the *means* of things. Have you never encountered a hard choice? Are all good things done only by irreproachably good people?

Hew glowered. He said, I don't understand why you don't just do something else. There are hundreds of very smart people working on high-temperature superconductivity. I believe you could solve it but do you really think you are *essential*? Let Zhou generalize ZEST. He'll figure it out.

Hew was trying to make me mad and had succeeded. I said: This is—this is the *point* of me. This is *my* problem. For forty years no one has been able to solve this and I really might solve it *if* I can work with Perry again. Yes he is a schmuck and he put us in a bad spot but for god's sake have a little perspective.

Hew said Okay, then stood and left the apartment.

He did not come back until pretty late. This gave the smog of my condescension some time to clear. Hew did remote IT support; actually he ran an IT team, was great at it. But, well, he was not at the vanguard of condensed-matter physics.

In the morning I tried a different pitch.

I said: Okay, think about it this way. Think about it like a *sacrifice*. The world cannot waste Perry. Who knows how much longer he will live?

I thought of the wheezing I could hear when Perry climbed the steps into the physics building; the arsenal of cardiovascular medications occupying half a cabinet in his kitchen.

Someone must make the next step, I said. It is too

important to leave undone or even to delay. The ice caps are melting. We submerge into this strange dark world, RIP, but temporarily! Then we return like Prometheus, bearing gifts, knowledge, an unfathomable boon of super-conductivity for all humanity. And if we go, if I can do it, no one *else* will have to go to Rape Island to solve HTS.

Hew said: Look, if you fail, we will never live it down. And if you succeed you will be validating the whole dis-gusting model of that place. You will make it so that awful backward men can forever claim that this perverse libertar-ian experiment is the *success* that gave us high-temperature superconductivity—and at a woman's hands, no less.

So be it.

There was one other thing that Hew demanded.

I want a moral offset. If we are going to the fucking Rubin Institute, if we are going to be complicit, we have *got* to go vegan.

6.

The ferry churned forward. The protesters' chants grew faint, vaguely pathetic, and soon disappeared behind us into the fog. We stood on the top deck facing into the chop of late-summer wind. I had been hungry for three weeks. I fantasized about cheeseburgers.

Hew tilted against the railing, swaying slightly with the boat's motion, his lips and cheeks pink in the summer sun. He was exceptionally thin—narrow forehead, sharp cheeks and chin and nose, a stomach that often seemed concave. But also he was tall, with wide shoulders. The first time I'd seen him I'd thought of him not as a person I desired but as a wiry structure I wished to climb. Presently I took his hand, for I was not above gratitude, and he kissed the top of my frizzy head. Then he detached his arm to wipe sea-spray from his glasses.

We were about a week late to the start of term. Astonishingly this had been no problem from a bureaucratic standpoint. Perry told someone that we were coming and would need housing, identification cards. Allegedly these issues were sorted. There had been only one form to sign to see all my academic credits, years of graduate study, seamlessly transferred into this new institutional framework. Another omnibus form covered health care, taxes, employment, liability waivers. I signed both on my phone. The ease of the whole thing felt amazing, felt *right*. Even Hew admitted the user experience was top-notch.

No cars were permitted on the island. It was small, a few square miles, with much of the land—the beaches, the cliffs, the forest—set aside for conservation. Walking was encouraged. When necessary, automated electric golf carts could be summoned by app, gratis. Accordingly we had sold our Subaru.

Plymouth Island resolved into view. It seemed almost to glow. Moist morning light refracted off Great Cliff, the rocky beaches, the immaculate lawns. The little town was all white-painted clapboard, black trim, gray shingles, sooty brick. Boats jostled and clinked in the marina.

Hew said, Oh my god.

Now, we had heard about this, had seen photos, but we did not expect—

Above all the quaintness loomed the throbbing center of the Institute: an enormous, rounded, beige tower. Its long shadow fell in a bold line across the academic pastures, the beach, even reaching the water. In the tower were offices, labs, classrooms, libraries, theaters, housing. (Also—a key feature of Perry's pitch—a 522-petaflop supercomputer on which we could *preempt* any project based outside the

Institute. No more *months* wasted *waiting* to run the simulation!!) To build a tower so large on an island so small, to root it deep in the island's brittle rock, this had taken marvelous and pricey engineering. It was unmistakably a phallus. It was known as the Endowment.

7.

Perry waited for us dockside. He was in fine form. Tan suit, straw trilby, Dr. Strangelove sunglasses, bow tie peppered with lacrosse sticks—his face *beaming*. He even embraced Hew, which must have been a first. For years they had been in a vaguely adversarial posture, each the other man in my life. Now I supposed Perry felt himself the gracious victor.

Perry set off striding through the cobblestoned town. It was picturesque, the shop windows manicured with bold-colored shutters. Before the Institute, the island had been mostly inns and art galleries and second homes for people priced out of Nantucket. Perry identified wonderful pastries here, mediocre sushi there.

Soon we ascended the hill and moved onto the campus proper. Oak-shaded paths wound through lawns so well-kept they looked artificial. Between heavy breaths Perry identified a former sea captain's house that was now the English department, another stately Victorian that was now Philosophy. He identified the homes of winners of various Nobels, the John Bates Clark Medal, the Fields Medal, the Pulitzer, the Best Director Oscar, the Bancroft Prize, the National Book Critics Circle Award, the Turner Prize. Here was the home of Senator Metzger, who had worn blackface in college, and the adjacent homes of three former Supreme Court justices. Over there, on a large grass ellipse, a Ponzi schemer completed a wobbly pass to an inside trader. There was the intern-fucker Vice President McMarmot, in a Hawaiian shirt, walking his labradoodle.

Hew said: Uh, Perry, we need to go back for our bags.

Perry laughed. Leave it to the porters!

Hew smiled uneasily.

Everything like that, said Perry, the *minutiae* of life, laundry, cleaning, it is all taken care of here! The dining rooms are quite exceptional for *cuisine institutionnelle*. Mario, the head chef, was once positively gilded in Michelin stars— but now he's ours, of course. The Institute is like Oxford in the good old days: they want to keep us engrossed in the *work* we are here to do.

Now Perry went on to identify the Greek Theater, where there was chamber music on temperate Fridays, and the staff dorm, whose visible element was two double doors to an elevator. The rest of the structure was underground, lit with artificial sunlight.

Meanwhile Hew's hand absolutely crushed around mine. He was taut as a trip wire. He was thinking that we had been here twenty minutes and already the place was corrupting us. Physically relocating to the Institute was one thing; it was another to accept the amenities.

Come in, come in, said Perry, at the door of his bungalow. We're having lunch.

On the patio lay a spread of Italian charcuterie, fragrant French cheeses, a duck pâté from Gascony. I wanted to die. And if Perry kept eating like this, I thought, he surely would. I tried to share a look with Hew but he remained in high tension, his face locked in a proctological stare.

Before I could waver toward the cheese Hew announced: Helen and I are vegans these days.

Ah, well! said Perry. Let me see what else they can do.

He got on the phone and declared to some unknown party, My guests are *vegan*! Can you—? Very good.

In the meantime Perry pushed bowls of olives, cornichons, and salted radishes in our direction. We drank wine. Within half an hour an autonomous golf cart arrived with a platter of lentil salad.

Hew was by now very agitated. The midday wine on an empty stomach had not helped things. Now Perry, he asked, with a feigned, almost British affect akin to Perry's own. How *does* a young, attractive woman, like, say, Helen here go about life on this island without being *constantly* harassed?

In other words: *En garde.*

Perry loved it. He said, Have you ever visited a prison?

I haven't, said Hew.

Well, I recommend it to you. It is *so* important for *so* many reasons to see how our society treats its criminals. But if we were on a prison tour together I would direct your attention to the gymnasium area.

Hew's face said, Okay . . .

The weight lifting equipment you will find there—the barbells, dumbbells, weight plates—will have all been purchased about thirty years ago. Yet, despite decades of constant use by supposedly lawless thugs, they will all be in immaculate condition. Do you know why?

Why don't you tell me, said Hew.

About thirty years ago, Perry said, a law was passed that precluded the introduction of *new* weight lifting equipment in federal prisons. The existing equipment became a scarce, nonrenewable resource. So it is treasured, treated with care. When there is a fight, all weights and dumbbells, conceivably quite *useful* in a brawl, are instantly set down, lest they be confiscated from the population forever.

Now, the Institute is about eighty percent men, Perry went on. And able female graduate students are the least common of all breeds. That situation is to no one's liking...

So I am a dumbbell, I said.

Well, I can hardly *vouch* for everyone, of course, said Perry, but I think you will find yourself handled rather delicately in most quarters. The hope is that women in your position might eventually report out, contra the zeitgeist, that the situation here is not *so* inhospitable after all.

Hew said, Okay, so what about all the macings?

This referred to several online videos of female Institute students whose unwanted advancers had apparently charged through every prior obstacle. The precise context of each incident could be hard to discern. But one could see, for instance, an increasingly agitated exchange beside a dining hall salad bar, an uninvited hand on the woman's arm, a lightning-fast draw, then the man argh-ing on the floor, covered in lettuce. To many these videos represented the generally oppressive and violent lived experience of women at RIP.

My own view was, How bad could it be?

In retrospect this might have been motivated reasoning. But I had thought I could model the social dynamics. At the Institute, I figured, there would be unusually aggressive men but also women who, having elected to come to RIP, were probably unusually confident in rebuffing or selecting among these advances. You would have bolder offense but also stronger defense. So maybe the dynamic would balance out? How different from real life could it be?

In any case, I did not expect the ordinary rules to apply to me. I had always been the intimidating un-girl; I was exceptional and expected to remain so. Moreover, in any case, when I was as intensely *focused* as I intended to be the *entire time* at RIP, I presented as kind of a lunatic. I could go about a week without showering before it bothered me. In high focus I traveled through corridors in either a hunched pounding charge or a loony meander, caressing the wall tiles while my mind hummed with code. It would take no extra work, in this condition, to persuade any man that I was not worth the effort, or so I then thought.

Regarding the videos, the macings, Perry said: Is there *data* reflecting that such things occur more frequently here than at other universities? They do happen elsewhere, yes? Or is the disproportionate public interest in these incidents *here* perhaps connected to the controversial ideology the Institute espouses?

Oh, data? Hew said. Let's discuss the data. Hew reached for his phone, prepared to whip out statistics.

I was not in the mood for a measuring contest. I said, Actually, let's go see our quarters. Thanks for lunch, Perry.

Hew and I walked toward the Endowment. Maybe I felt more than the usual number of eyes on me? There *were* a lot of men around. Even compared to Cornell, I noted a surplus of boat shoes and khaki. Two of the women I saw were wearing pearls; the third wore huge headphones. Hew kept stewing. He wanted to have it out. He grumbled, Don't know why I'm surprised, but Perry obviously likes it here. That guy is a *true believer*.

8.

The Endowment was peak design, rugged steel, polished concrete, triple-pane glass. Environmental certifiers begrudgingly certified it at the highest tier of sustainable construction. The key architectural feature was the dense round spine at the tower's center. This plunged about a thousand feet into the rock below, with the rest of the building basically hanging off it. The spine encased the elevators, and its particular physics, its engineering, would in light of what came later become a subject of significant popular interest.

We were escorted to the seventeenth floor. Our apartment—open plan, sweeping views, custom fixtures, a heated bidet toilet seat—was not what the term "graduate housing" typically brings to mind.

I unpacked. Hew patrolled uselessly, his arms cinched across his diaphragm. He kept touching light switches, opening and shutting soft-close cabinets. He said, I really do not feel good. I'm just disgusted by this whole place.

He said, The students here aren't students—they're prey.

It is not forever.

Oh, he said. Approximately how long do you think it will take you to solve high-temperature superconductivity and save the planet?

Approximately how many more times would you like to have this argument? The good—

The *potential* good.

Fine, the *potential* good offsets the bad.

Just tell me what it would take for you to give up. What would make you cut your losses?

Would you please—

No, seriously, Hew said. Can you at least ballpark it? Give me something to hold out for.

Well, a PhD is *supposed* to take five or six years. I'm at five.

So, one year?

In one year, we can reassess.

Okay, he said, and having won this symbolic, inchoate concession finally seemed to relax for the first time all day.

We are not the problem, Hew. *I* am not the problem. Can you get on my team? Or at least deal with those boxes? I pointed into the kitchen.

He looked around at all there was to do, all the unpacking and arranging, and finally smiled. Chores were not chores to him. I funneled my whole life at physics, all hassles and distractions banished. But chores were almost treats for Hew—clear chances to set something tangibly aright. He had a semirural WASP background, big on self-reliance, not big on comparative advantage. Plus I suppose the barrage of silly questions Hew fielded in his job left him particularly determined never to ask for such assistance himself. Back in our rickety duplex in Ithaca, he was constantly fixing things. I would come home from lab at 10 p.m. and find our kitchen sink deconstructed, Hew cross-legged on the floor, watching plumbing videos on his phone. An hour later he would plop on the couch and announce, very casually, leaking immense pride: Done, just saved us a call to the super.

Hew took to unpacking. After a minute he came over and wrapped his arms around my hips. At first I didn't really want him to touch me, but still I leaned back into his hands, letting them hold me. I'm sorry, he said. Hew liked to fix things and so he knew how to apologize. I never had to wrench it out of him. He always seemed to mean it.

9.

The semester took off. I was back behind the wheel of my life. I was at work.

Perry and I caught each other up on all the missteps we had made separately, combined them into an enormous consolidated hunk of mistakes, then began to chisel and cure. Sometimes we were side by side on parallel terminals in lab, down in the dense cool underfloors of the Endowment. Sometimes we were at his bungalow, or in his office on the thirtieth floor.

But mostly I was alone. I found it was, actually, easier to focus when one availed oneself of every convenience. The kitchen made these organic breakfast bars—a robot delivery cart brought a stack to me every morning, along with a carafe of Ethiopian coffee. At lunch, when I remembered to eat it, my desk filled with plates of pita, garlic hummus, Sichuan-oil beet dip, and walnut-radicchio salad. Twice daily my dishes were cleared, my trash was emptied, my terminal was dusted, and my desk chair was tucked in by someone I never saw and rarely thought about, for I was in my element. Real life was inside the model.

Sometimes I would be on the elevator up to see Hew, or I would be on the toilet, and would suddenly see my way through a thicket. Then it was DoorCloseDoorClose DoorClose, back down to lab before it escaped me.

Sometimes I would be alone in lab, chipping, whittling, writing, rewriting. Then there, in an email from Perry, would be this *pristine* phrase of code—or a single sentence, no further explanation offered or needed—and with this piece in place a mass of convoluted structures would collapse like Tetris, unnecessary. There is no better feeling in computational physics than confidently discarding a huge amount of prior work.

Meanwhile I was neglecting Hew even more than usual. More than was prudent. From the outset of our relationship, in that first conversation back in Ithaca in which Hew had told me that he would like to be with me if I would have him, I had said: You should be aware, my attempts at being a girlfriend have not met with universal acclaim. Do you *really* understand what I'm like?

You have a calling, he said.

You can't try to compete, I said. I won't like it. Basically you will get scraps of my attention, most of the time. Others have found that insufficient.

Some part of me was trying to scare him off. But then Hew cracked me, saying something along the lines that I was the rare person who knew what she wanted and that he admired me and my self-sufficiency and my purpose and that he wanted to be with such a person, where I would really have my own life of the mind, and that of course he would not want to interfere with my work, which he said he knew was globally important, and that he would respect my work regardless, even if it wasn't globally important, simply because it was mine.

Easier said than sustained, of course. I don't doubt he tried, even after we got to the Institute. I probably could have been less absent than I was.

For weeks, I left early and Hew woke up alone in our immaculate apartment, this luxurious capillary of a great repugnant schlong of a building. The furniture, appliances, and finishes were all terribly functional; the place's salient character was what it had cost. In my absence he toggled between his work—numbing team videoconferences, remotely burping tech hiccups—and immersing himself, to a high degree even for him, in being Online. Unbeknownst to me he was becoming more active on threads, forums, news feeds. When he could no longer stand it in our apartment, he jogged around campus, horrifying himself.

The impunity. The apparent normalcy of life at a university that was *emphatically* not normal. Hew watched preppy girls moving queenlike across the lawns, thirsty boys reliably wafting behind them. He watched undergraduates flow into William F. Buckley Hall for one of the Institute's notorious required courses, The Canon—the syllabus for which included dead white men only, and the professor for which had opposed affirmative action at Berkeley because it would "dilute" the talent pool. Hew would eat, fuming, in the humblest of the dining halls, which nonetheless was all marble and bronze and beside the salad bar had a station that daily offered some ostentatiously problematic meat: foie gras, roast suckling pig, octopus, horse.

In the Endowment atrium, Hew watched faculty who should have been stripped of all life's pleasures gather for daily afternoon tea. In general, the tea was a traditional English affair—watercress-and-cucumber sandwiches, staff in starched formal wear, etc. But on Wednesdays, Englishness gave way to other cultures. One week, Wednesday tea had been "Oriental": oolong, moon cakes, the staff in qipaos and Nehru jackets. Another week, Moroccan: mint tea, the staff in silk vests and fezzes. Egyptian tea featured belly dancers.

I was functionally oblivious to all this. For a while, the closest I came to meeting a stranger was one evening: I was on my way up from lab and the elevator stopped on the library floor. A young woman walked in. She was South Asian, very slight, and wore no makeup. She was pretty and had studious hair, big and oily, like mine. She clutched an organic chemistry textbook cluttered with tabs.

Hi, she said.

Hi, I said.

The point seemed to be to acknowledge that we were both, improbably, women. We rode up the shaft of the Endowment regarding each other in the gold-rimmed mirror of the elevator door.

When I came into our apartment, Hew was horizontal on the couch. He had some medical show on but was reading his phone.

This girl I saw, what's someone like her doing here? I said. You know...woman of color, no pearls, studying chemistry. Do you think it's Ayn Rand by day, science by night?

Oh, not necessarily.

You think she had no other options?

Hew then explained to me how, beneath the Institute's trollish shell, thirty to forty percent of students were not here for its cause but for its funding. These were smart kids whose parents were nurses and truck drivers, for whom the debt attached to any regular school looked insane compared to the stringless free ride the Institute offered. These students scurried between classes; they ate in the offscreen nooks of the dining halls; they convened in their dorm rooms, not in the palatial lounges with the diamond-stud and boat-shoe kids. Hew muttered about how without these students RIP would be a summer camp, utterly unserious as an intellectual endeavor, and yet these students had to live like a cowering underclass...

10.

Hew grew fixated on the man responsible.

Not Perry. The real man responsible, the Institute's visionary and benefactor and President, was the eponymous Buckminster Witherspoon Rubin.

B.W. Rubin lived on the top floors of the Endowment, with his offices on the floors immediately below. He was not a recluse, but RIP was just one of his many going concerns; thus he was not exactly loitering around campus, greeting newcomers. B.W. was sometimes glimpsed but rarely met. This reinforced the mysterious power that seemed to emanate from his name, his distant form.

Now, one did not have to stalk B.W. as thoroughly as Hew did to know that he had been born at the confluence of two nontrivial fortunes, and that he had transformed this mere billion-dollar kernel into around $95 billion in less than twenty years. Then he had been evicted from BWR Capital for reasons not precisely known. Probably it was a scandal of some sort, people suspected. Indeed it must have been *rather* bad, people suspected, for him to be chucked from the company where he had earned such astonishing returns for so many satisfied investors.

These suspicions seemed corroborated when, after leaving BWR Capital, he had immediately founded this Institute whose entire countercultural ideology was that it did not care at all about personal behavior, *only* about whether you operated in your vocation with excellence. The Institute had no committees; B.W. alone decided who became faculty, and the key qualifications were thought to be some high level of professional achievement combined with intolerance for—*ideally* some history of conflict with—what B.W. once called "faculty lounge neopuritan Maoists." The Institute remained governed by the laws of the State of Connecticut. But it was distinguished as about the only well-funded institution in America with no internal regulations layered on top of the law. Indeed it was not clear whether actual crimes, even prison time, would cause one to lose one's position at RIP.

The whole enterprise was a provocation, of course. B.W. built the Endowment to specifications that allowed him, on a clear day, from a telescope in his office, to look toward the northwest horizon and gaze *down* at Yale. He invited astonished reporters to visit, enjoy the view.

So it repulsed Hew on every level: there was the despicable social ideology of RIP, but almost as vile was the robber-baron personal wealth that made the place possible. Hew began to obsess over B.W. the way one obsesses over the source of a foul odor in the kitchen. B.W.'s moral stench seemed, to Hew, to be dripping down on us from twenty-five stories up. It had drenched the whole island. It had to be eradicated.

Needless to say Hew was not making any friends. He slept minimally, and more than once I woke up for the bathroom at 3 a.m. to find him still at his desk, trawling the #RIPRIP forums. He basically refused to speak to anyone besides me. At the few meals we ate together in the dining halls, I saw him glaring at anyone who appeared to be enjoying themselves. I noticed him watching women, the undergraduates especially, with a parental protective focus, alert to signs of distress, eager for a glance that would beg him, an *ally,* to intervene. In short he was getting fairly deranged. But it was hard to know what to do about it, seeing as I had insisted on this deranging environment.

Then one day B.W. came to my lab.

I have never been able to say precisely what it is about bankers' clothes that communicates price. It is not a uniform that obviously permits fashion; you would think blazers are blazers, slacks are slacks, loafers are loafers, but no. Something about the cut, the *new*ness, told me these items would wipe out an entire term's graduate stipend. Or maybe there was nothing special about the clothes. Maybe it was the fact of his wealth, my *knowledge* of that fact, that lent B.W.'s clothes this nimbus of quality.

He stood in the doorway, silhouetted because I preferred to work in almost-dark. He was so rich his face was essentially featureless; the money was all you could think about. What I discerned was that he was not tall, not handsome, did not wear glasses. When he moved forward into my screenglow I could see his nose's open pores.

Uh, Mr. Rubin, I said.

It's B.W., please.

Perry isn't here.

Yes, I wanted to see you, Helen. How's the food? he asked solicitously.

What?

You have various dietary restrictions, I believe.

I had not told him my name, never mind about veganism. Perry was such a talker, though.

The food's fine, I said. I haven't starved.

I talked to Mario. Soon you'll have more options. You'll tell the kitchen what you like. They can make anything.

Okay, I said. Thanks.

I might have smiled? Right or wrong, this was a consequential man. For some reason he had come to the basement to talk to me. It seemed like he wanted me to understand that he was doing me a favor.

He said, Perry claims you are getting close on high-temperature superconductors.

That's very hard to say.

Suppose you *had* to say, Helen.

He was now standing beside my terminal, directly above me, his tone conspiratorial.

I said, We're making progress.

How can I help? I will dump money on this problem if you tell me where to back up the truck. What do you need that you do not already have?

Five more of me, maybe.

B.W. did not laugh. He said: So you need research assistants. How many would you like?

Oh god, no, I said. Really we need to be left alone.

For a moment, all the theatricality left his face. B.W. stared at me like I was a sudoku, an asset he was valuing.

Do you know where I live? he said.

I pointed at the ceiling.

If you think of anything you need, come up. My door is open to you.

Okay.

Adieu, he said, then B.W. departed as abruptly as he had arrived. I listened to his tasseled loafers stride away. As I was gathering my things to go upstairs and tell Hew that I had *met* B.W. Rubin, I realized that Perry had *completely* botched our representation of Cooper pairing in a doped Mott insulator. Unless this was rewritten wholesale our model would fail to populate the output vector, and unless I did this before Perry resumed work in the a.m. we would just create more cleanup for ourselves later.

Accordingly I did not get back upstairs until late. Hew was asleep in his eye mask, which meant Do Not Disturb Even If You Have Just Met the King of All Billionaire Schmucks.

11.

A few days later Hew and I managed to have sex for the first time in five or six or maybe ten weeks. Certainly for the first time since we'd arrived at RIP. We were not a sexless maybe-marriage but sometimes this fact felt like a technicality. We no longer had a sexual habit. Or I guess our habit was generally to refrain. But external forces could still act upon us. I could go weeks without thinking about it, noticing my body only when it obstructed thought, but then Jupiter's moons would come into alignment. Neptune would enter the Seventh House or something, and I would brush by Hew in the hallway and feel a tickle of desire. I wanted to climb those shoulders and smear his chest against mine. I wanted his long strong legs twined in my legs.

The question then became: How to invite him, or incite him? I needed to warm Hew out of his morose, brooding mind-set. A delicate task. I had to be deliberate, but if it was too calculated the process would not work for either of us. Neptune would downsize from the Seventh House to a sensible condominium and Hew and I would find our way into some petty argument.

It was a fine afternoon. Toasted clouds conveyed themselves across a vast horizon; the ocean looked glazed. I'd had an exceptionally productive morning. What are you doing now? I asked Hew. Are you busy?

He shrugged. What are you thinking?

Maybe let's cook something, I said. This was not exactly a euphemism but it would be, I knew, a symbolically charged suggestion. Cooking together was a lot like sex for us. We had done it very often in our first fresh years of coupledom, but the necessary astrological mood now less and less often struck us. We had not cooked once since arriving at RIP. I'd been working incessantly, and neither of us would be facile with vegan cooking, and the obscene availability of prepared food from the Institute dining halls—and the ease of having it delivered—had inverted the economics of our lifestyle. Now a project as elaborate and time-hungry as cooking felt perversely luxurious. Back at Cornell, takeout was not quite a special occasion but had to be done sparingly.

Are we—Hew laughed. Are we even *allowed* to cook for ourselves? Isn't that frowned on?

Oh right, I said, I guess we wouldn't want to cause offense.

There was a small but well-stocked market in town next to the Two Scoop Creamery. We got sorbet and then purchased the ingredients for homemade pasta, a Hew specialty, plus beautiful fall vegetables still smudged with organic local soil. Hew's demeanor on our outing remained somber and obliging until, finally, on the walk back up toward the Endowment, he took my hand. *There,* I thought. *There* is my Hew. With the crinkle of the paper grocery bag jostling against his chest, his fingers like a warm wire basket around mine, the brisk fall breeze, I'm sure we both felt we were back in Ithaca.

Watching him activate our kitchen brought my desire to more than a tickle. His big shoulders and hands pulsed in the dough. In so much of his life Hew had become uptight and meticulous, but the way he made pasta was still instinctive. He hardly measured his ingredients; combining the flours, the water, the salt, tasting, adjusting, until the texture was right. Meanwhile I remained glued to my recipe, as always, precisely measuring every spice, making a show of doing this because Hew thought it was funny.

With a chopstick, I nudged a single grain of salt toward a tiny salt pile on the cutting board. Then I stood back and announced: Perfect.

What's perfect?

Exactly one pinch.

I'll give you exactly one pinch, he said, clacking his tongs.

Soon the apartment swarmed with the scents of oil and garlic and onion, and though we had no meat on the premises I was feeling carnivorous—but also heartsore. Memory was intruding. Maybe there is something dangerous in too successfully re-creating happier times? Human lives typically do not look best in sharp relief. I thought about how one time Hew and I had passed a guy on the street in Ithaca whose shirt announced that THE FUTURE IS FEMALE.

Hew had smirked. It might as well say PRETTY PLEASE TOUCH MY VIRTUOUS PENIS.

Needless to say, this kind of humor was nowadays as unthinkable for Hew as a future that was not female.

At the beginning of it all—the great awakening, the movement, the purge—I would tease Hew, prodding him to tell me what he expected to get canceled for. This was, I maintain, a joke. But at the same time, if there was something worth knowing, I did want to know it. They *will* come for you eventually, I said. And I'll have to stand by you despite whatever it is. So it would be decent to give me a *hint*?

Well, all right, Hew said. He stroked his chin ponderously. Your clue is: human trafficking.

Another time he said, Your clue is: Armenian genocide.

But Hew pretty soon lost his cool. Probably I was too persistent. One time while we were cooking risotto, I jokingly, or so I thought, said: Give me another hint.

He snapped, You know, it kind of bothers me that you keep asking. Do you actually suspect I've done something?

I dropped it. I was, for a moment, sure that Hew *had* done something to be sorry about.

Later that same night, we were in bed. This was back before sex was a special occasion. I slid off him and we lay side by side. I felt the cool air on my lower back and his damp chest slowing with sleep, briefly, and then awake again. There was no moon and our always-dark Ithaca bedroom was especially so.

Quietly this time, he said: Do you actually think I might have done something, you know...like what these other guys did?

The evening air wafted with sweat and candor. I said, It seems...not impossible. I don't think you would, but really how would I know? I've seen enough cop shows not to want to be the killer's blindsided, tearful spouse. She always looks like such a dope.

Spouse? Anyway I think that's what bothers me, he said.

That I could contemplate you as a rapist and murderer?

No, what really bothers me is that...I don't know either. Even *I* don't know whether I've done anything wrong.

I twined my fingers into his hair.

I would...Hew said. His voice trailed off, plaintive in the pitch dark.

He said: I would just really like someone to tell me what's going on. What are the rules now? I feel sure there was a time when I could tell you with some confidence whether I had ever done anything very seriously wrong. Something gravely immoral. Now I don't know. I'm just waiting to be accused of something. My only certainty is that I do not currently understand my past the way I will eventually understand it. Have women been unhappy with me? Have I had bad sex, said careless things? Yes. With you, even. With you most of all. But have I done something reprehensible? How would I know it if I did? Perhaps I *just now* committed a serious offense and *neither* of us knows it. We're a couple. I didn't ask for affirmative consent. But should I have? Should I have asked for express consent the first time we ever slept together? I don't think I did it then either—but we didn't miscommunicate, did we?

No, we didn't, I said. My heart was veal. Hew was an emotional creature but was rarely so vulnerable, even with me.

He said: I feel like we've all been shoved into a chute. We don't know where we're going and our memories, almost our whole identities, have not been erased so much as . . . nullified. I have some idea what the *facts* are but I don't know what any of it *means*. I don't know what was *significant*.

You're bewildered, you mean.

Something more than usual seems predetermined, doesn't it? It's like that play—I can't remember the name—the one where the coin comes up heads a hundred times running. If you play at all, you know the result. Heads, heads, heads. And maybe that is what they will always want: our heads. Maybe everyone is guilty. Certainly I *feel* guilty. I feel like I *must* have done something bad, at least arguably. I almost want to be accused—just to know the accusation. I want to confess to something, but to what?

I nuzzled my head onto his shoulder. I knew that if Hew did have a confession, he would now be making it.

Hew sighed satirically, melodramatically. He said, I know how I'll solve this. I'll make myself a shirt: PLEASE CANCEL ME.

Now, that will show the FUTURE IS FEMALE guys who means business.

Or maybe it should say, I'M FUCKING PETRIFIED.

The thing, though, was that Hew really was petrified. Like probably a lot of men, he was at sea. For a while he was searching for high ground and in the scramble upward basically radicalized himself. He could not live indefinitely with such intense moral suspense, such uncertainty about his own place. To know himself again he became the sort of man who would never, could never. Even then I thought it was to his credit that he took his own ethics so seriously.

But at the same time it was pretty annoying, pretty performative. I kept waiting for the whole thing to die down. Of course as a woman I did not suffer such an extreme paradigm shift. I didn't have to be quite as defensive; I was presumed to be more or less on the right side, at least re gender—and I think I was on the right side, more or less?

What made me an outlier in our college town was not my politics but how little I thought about politics. My great privilege was to work in a field that had essentially nothing to do with human beings. So I pretty quickly lost interest in the new wokeness dawning elsewhere. I figured that either these new values would fade away or they would become normalized, but regardless they would soon become as uninteresting to everyone else as they already were to me. And in the meantime, I expected that few men in my field would ever be seriously sidetracked by the discourse. Ideas, models, experiments in physics— they worked or they didn't; not much subjectivity was involved. So I could not afford to lose focus. I thought politics would never make much difference in my own personal life. Maybe if I had not been so busy, I would have heard the gods laughing in the distance.

While our pasta dough dried, Hew made us martinis. I watched as he made them both dry, with a twist, instead of making mine dirty with a pile of olives, the way he knew I preferred. This was either obliviously inconsiderate or a passive-aggressive refusal to accommodate me in this instance while he was accommodating me in so many larger ways. I knew I shouldn't have, that I ought not retaliate with my own indifference, but as he presented my glass on the counter, I pulled out my laptop.

Now we're working? Hew said.

Sorry, I just need to fix one thing, before I forget. It's been nagging at me.

Then Hew got on his phone for a while.

We ate by the window, our attitudes stiff and cold. We watched the long shadow of the Endowment fade into dusk, and my irritation faded too. I became determined that we would not let distraction or annoyance, my own momentary pettiness, defeat what I believed we had both set out to do. Hew was agreeable when I extended my leg under the table to rest it on his thigh. So finally we consummated the evening. The sex was rote, essentially mechanical, a form of exercise. As exercise it was more like a treadmill than, say, tennis.

Still, it did clear out the synapses. My head on his panting chest, I was not for a moment thinking of code or better times. He was not so buttoned up. His hand caressed my spine and he looked at me with open if slightly desperate affection. One of the perverse by-products of my general emotional absence was that engagement, when I managed even a little, could be very potent for him. More than once I had ended days-long arguments through mere application of attention.

Hew said, I have got to get off this island for a while.

It might do you good.

It might do you good too. There's an action at Penn next weekend.

I knew what he was thinking: attend a rally, shout our values, cleanse our souls. But, well, I was not the protesting type. I had gone to maybe three ever. Each time—despite in fact disliking economic inequality, sexual harassment, and racialized police brutality—I had felt crushingly self-conscious, completely unlike myself. I fumbled through the chants and hugs of solidarity like an actor who has forgotten her lines, and at the end I felt just as humiliated. Hew knew this, of course. He must have expected me to decline. I said: I can't. We are cleaning up the model next week.

What is a few days? he said.

We are really close to being able to *run* this puppy. Just not a great week to lose momentum.

Do you mind if I go? I dunno, I really need some society.

Go, of course, I said. This week is shot for me. We would hardly see each other anyway.

12.

When he was alone, which is to say after my mom died, my dad got a little weird. He lost balance. Jewishness became salient. Americanness became salient. Maybe this was who he always would have been, absent the gentle gentile he'd married. He left his law firm, insisting to me, though I was only twelve and could not really have been expected to disagree, that he would do better under his own shingle.

The firm has *conflicts,* he explained. The firm takes a cut. But my clients do not come for the firm; they come for *yours truly.*

His line of work was representing small companies in disputes with their insurers.

Many of these companies did, after all, come for the firm. Dad had been anxious about the need for staff, for infrastructure; how many employees would he require to handle the torrent of paper? One part-time secretary, as it turned out. Dad was not busy. He did not mind. It left more time for reading.

Mostly he read history. The Soviet Union had vanished some years prior, but the literature on the causes of its demise, the disease it had been carrying from the outset, continued to flow onto the long shelves of our basement bookcases. My dad's particular concern was the argument, advanced quietly but unmistakably in WASP foreign affairs commentary, that the communist disease had at the beginning been invented, carried, and communicated by Jews.

It could not be denied that Marx and Trotsky were Jewish, and Lenin in part, nor that Jews had been overrepresented among the old Bolsheviks and Soviet elite. But!, my dad wrote in numerous letters to the editor, if you are going to fault Jews for being such good communists you must also credit them for being such excellent Americans! Moreover, hasn't the entire global economy shifted from agriculture to services and manufacturing? Hasn't the *whole modern world* become mobile, multilingual, financial, transactional? In other words, *are we not all now doing what Jews used to do?*

He could really go on about this. By the time I hit high school, I made a point not to listen. Dad was Jewish enough that he could not bring himself to interrupt a child doing homework, and this was how I defended myself. Another way I defended myself was by being, from thirteen to sixteen, a pretty huge bitch to him. Finally I defended myself with a strategic retreat, an early departure to college.

Dad was religious, though not in the sense of liking religion. He did not attend synagogue or study the Talmud. The ideal he worshipped was the consummate pluralist, the assimilated American Jew. He worshipped the American who was fully American, perfectly American, *because* of his Jewishness. The American identity was not complete without some ethnic particularity—this was a *necessary element*—but of course it must take the right form. It must be of the right scale. You could not be Hasidic, for instance, and be completely perfectly American. You could not be a Zionist, a devotee of another nation-state, and be completely perfectly American. You had to be an individualist, a capitalist; probably you had to love baseball. You had to *use* the liberty the Founders had given you.

The great rabbi of my dad's religion was Leopold Lens. He was a novelist, a satirist, an iconoclast. He had used his liberty, famously, with hundreds of women. Lens was a scholar of cultural ambivalence. He was allergic to ideology, to purity. He was, my dad emphasized, an *unremittingly independent* thinker, and it was only through this independence, this refusal to be pinned in any one place, that one could be both as American and as Jewish as my dad wished to be. Besides history, Dad read only Lens and a few other writers whom Lens himself admired. For years Dad had been emailing me Lens excerpts. A typical Subject line: "More magic from the Maestro."

I had, in high school, read one of the shorter novels and said, in the most casual possible concession, that it was funny. From this Dad inferred that we had this *profound shared love* of Lens, that *this* was the common ground on which he could meet his daughter. Certainly we did not have much else to talk about, so I let it go on. But in truth I read very little Lens besides that one novel and the excerpts Dad sent me, which I would digest only enough to feign appreciation. Sometimes I insinuated that I too had been awed by the very same passage when I read it as part of my own independent course of Lens study.

Anyway the Institute did not keep a central directory, or if it did I had never encountered it.

Therefore I had no reason to expect to encounter Leopold Lens.

Hew had left for Philadelphia by way of New York. Perry and I had that morning *finished our model;* it was sparkling. Perry had proposed a bundle of new concepts and as our numericist I had figured out how to make our code not just coherent but swift. We would test several hypotheses at once. We knew the model would not *work*—we knew it would not actually accurately simulate HTS—but I had gotten it to a state that justified running it on a super-computer. This was no small thing. Usually you have to wait months or years between supercomputer simulations. These computers are extremely rare, and physicists have to share them with everyone else—with computational biologists, economists, computer scientists, etc. But all Perry and I had to do was wait a *few days* for some biochemists to finish with the Institute's supercomputer, then run our simulation, which would take only 181 hours (!!!) at 522 petaflops. The ways in which our model failed to replicate actual experimental data would tell us what to try next.

Perry said, Come over, we'll have dinner before the party.

I said, What party?

My god, Helen, you have been working too hard. The

Lucretius Festival. The fall party. There are signs every-where. The entire Institute is invited to—

For the first time since arriving on the island, I wore a dress. I *was* feeling festive: the model ready, an unexpected party. Also relevant: Hew out of town. He had been such a handbrake lately that it was hard not to feel his absence as a relief. I straightened my hair and shaved my legs. I am small but not squat, nominally but not impressively thin. I have made no notable modifications to my default settings. My face is tight and direct, though my cheeks can do a cherub thing, and I am plausibly but not distinctively Jewish. With a little mascara my eyes can be interest-ing. My hair is irremediably huge. That night I wore a silver-and-lapis necklace Hew had gotten for me in one of his rare, but always successful, forays into jewelry. My dress had thin straps, and I covered my shoulders with a howling-orange tasseled shawl, which floated behind me as I crossed campus.

Then, in Perry's living room, Leopold Lens.

He stood when I entered. He was tall, which surprised me. He did not smile, really, but extended a hand and said, I'm Leo and you are Helen.

Yes, I said.

He held the handshake for the exact right amount of time. His gaze lingered, or at least I thought it did. It was probing, not lascivious. He had this vaguely Roman nose, bold brows, and a blizzard of gray hair. His hair was vital and incongruous, as enticing as a beauty mark on a model's cheek. I felt like I was checking on each of his features, proofreading his face for mistakes that would tell me, No, this is *not* Leopold Lens. You are *not this moment* face-to-face with *the Maestro*.

Okay! Perry said, emerging from the kitchen with a tray of cocktails. Good, you've met. Leo is a writer.

I've heard, I said. I've even read.

Have you really? Perry said. Leo, you should be awfully flattered by that. Helen here is one of the great minds of her generation; she has a reasonable chance of saving the world from climate change. But she is, forgive me, a *tad myopic*. She is not exactly *plugged* into the culture.

Well, that is exactly why she's heard of me.

The men ate quail. I ate what I always now ate at Perry's: roasted vegetables, lentil salad, sourdough. Perry kept them around for me, my presence in the bungalow being frequent but unpredictable.

I explained that Hew was off at an action in Philadelphia.

Leo Lens smirked: An *action*! What a perfectly vacant description. Something will occur, is what that tells you. Whoever named your generation had foresight, Helen.

What do you mean?

Before your generation assumed the label, to be "millennial" meant to transcend all suffering, to redeem all sin—to enter an era of human perfection. In other words it meant to herald apocalyptic change. And as it turns out this is *precisely* what your millenarian cohort intends.

So I suppose your "cohort" never intended to improve things? That explains a lot, actually.

Leo Lens grinned. Perry grinned.

Leo went on, Most of us had religion to keep us sane.

I did not think you were a fan, I said.

For myself, no, I'm not really. I never was. But seeing what has happened to your peers, Helen, *without* a little organized religion—

I think atheism is one of their great generational *achievements*, said Perry. They are confirmation for the rest of us: the nays have it.

That is an illusion, said Leo. He ate a macaroon. Her generation *thinks* they are not religious. They *think* there has never been a more secular or rational American generation—except that religion is everywhere once you are looking for it. Even in the semantics, how they talk to each other. People are woke like they are saved. Don't you see, wokeness is a theology? But a theology with no text, no god, no organizing myth or principles, no traditions. There is in this millennial religion only the vaguest sense of good and evil, applied to daily life by an ever-shifting clergy of popular priests and priestesses. On their phones at all hours, they "follow" the priest *du jour,* absorbing the gospel, then some find a new priest, schism, then schism again. They *do have* a religion: it is the religion of the mob.

To all of this I thought: Well, duh. Quite obviously this is what Leopold Lens would think.

Shortly we headed out to the party.

13.

The party centered in the atrium of the Endowment and spilled onto the lawn beneath strings of lights and electric heaters. Like the Wednesday teas, the event was culturally maximalist and flagrantly appropriative. Two Black women in dirndls served German biers; tacos came from a white man in a poncho and sombrero; two kimono-clad East Asian women would bow while handing you sashimi. An eighteen-piece band played Sinatra. The waitstaff circulated in scanty togas.

I watched a film critic ogle the woman collecting his empty champagne flute, then realized that my own choice of dress had implications too. Ditto the orange shawl, the lipstick. For nearly two months I had been darting between semiprivate spaces thoroughly unconcerned with how I presented, which was how I usually liked to present. Suggesting vagrancy was a good way to be left alone, thus my normal appearance said: Try me. But tonight my appearance said: Try me! Even compared to years in STEM, this crowd was astonishingly male and white. It was jarring to see everyone in one place like this. I was a magnet passing shreds of foil; hundreds of eyes affixed, rotating to follow me. Many of the other women had known better; they were wearing big sweaters and pantsuits.

Perry vanished almost immediately. Suboptimal, I thought.

I was not with Hew, did not have a possessive arm to cling to. Instead I was in line at the bar beside Leo Lens, the apparent meaning of which did not escape me. It was saying I was the sort of young woman who went places with Leo Lens. He had been famous as a novelist— but still, not so famous that one would have expected him to go around with Goldie Hawn and then Kathleen Turner, as he had in fact done. Other men, and perhaps other women, gave him a certain kind of credit for this. Now I could feel how Lens's body language, the way he leaned into me, was gently but distinctly proprietary. I could hear libidinal gears spinning all around us, process- ing that here was a young woman who did not mind an older man.

For the first but not the last time, Leo seemed to be reading my mind. Or at least he could discern that I was uncomfortable and that this had something to do with the gender ratio. He said: Why are you at the Institute, Helen?

I told him. Perry was *sui generis.*

Now you, I said.

Isn't it obvious? Leo said.

It's not, actually. If you'd had a public trial, I think I

would have heard about it. But I had no idea you were in exile.

I was not forced out, he said, though some tried. For decades, Leo had been the preeminent (and then formerly preeminent) member of the faculty at a writing program in the Catskills.

He said, We had the thought police, armed with hair-trigger bullhorns, the same as everywhere. Allegedly I hated women, hated Jews, though I rarely had complaints from women or Jews who knew me. Nonetheless, I was ostracized. I would like to say I didn't mind but... well, I did. Lens shrugged, almost embarrassed, and in his eyes I saw something I did not expect—melancholy.

All of this started years ago. But then this Institute sprang into being. The values of *this* place, Leo said, gesturing around, they actually suit me. At least in the abstract. At least in part. Of course there were practical considerations too: Better money here, and no teaching. A no-brainer for me. I did not have much ivory tower approval left to lose.

I see, I said. Well then, what about the Institute does *not* suit you?

I suspect it's the same thing that does not suit you: the paucity of women. Now, do not misunderstand me. My erotic life is *kaput*. I was never quite the Lovelace everyone seemed to think I was, but now I've become at long last one of those elderly fellows who really has learned to behave correctly. Nonetheless, without women, my world is out of balance. It is the charged *conversation* I lust after — the *waltz* of it.

I thought: What Dad would do to be here instead of me! Through dinner with Lens and Perry I had felt the usual lite frustration, the vague disgust one grows accustomed to around pompous men. But now that we were wandering through the party, one-to-one, away from the buffeting winds of Perry's ego, there was something softer about Lens, something gelatinous and mesmerizing. It was in the lilt and flow and paragraph structure of Lens's speech and the unrepressed comfort with which he said "erotic," a word that Hew and I had probably never said to one another. It was in his regal gait; in the intense yet comfortable quality of his eye contact; in the way he turned his whole torso, not just his head, to look at me. Lens had a physical ease about him—perhaps a metaphysical ease? In contrast of course to Hew, whose back and shoulders felt like an exoskeleton.

Leo said: The Institute has not turned out quite how some envisioned. There were many who hoped to turn the clock back to the universities of the sixties and the seventies. To the era of free love, when students had the capacity to consent to fucking their professors, and often did so. This place was pitched as an *intellectual* orgy but some, I believe, hoped for simply an orgy.

Which they have not been having, I take it.

The clock wound back too far for them, to that era when faculties were almost all men and students were almost all men and the range of sexual opportunities suited only the Oxford types like Perry.

Perry does love it here, doesn't he?

Leo looked puzzled, along the lines of No shit. He said, Well, yes. And in saying no more he made me sure I had missed something.

I said: You know, I don't really mind it. In a strange way this is an amazing place for a woman to get work done. You sort of *must* ignore everything else.

Absolutely correct, Leo said. If you get defensive about the Institute, your work will atrophy. You will fixate on trivialities of local culture. When in fact there is nothing strange going on: everyone here is like everyone everywhere else. We are all just living in the world, day by day, accepting the best offers available to us.

My partner feels like we're living in a sewer.

Hence the *action* in Philadelphia. An ethical shower.

I guess, I said.

We were now outside the Endowment, under the strings of lights and the heat lamps. The air smelled electric, like autumn and white wine. It was undeniably a romantic setting. I was noticing things I didn't usually notice, like the color of Lens's hazel eyes and the drape of his shirt and pleated slacks. I wondered how one broached the topic that one's father is obsessed with one's new acquaintance. For a while we walked quietly together. We brushed by a podcaster who had defended his theoretical right to use the N-word when quoting song lyrics. He was talking to a classicist who had actually used the N-word and meant it. Beside them was an Asian American woman, a law professor who often went on TV to defend the police after they'd shot a person of color. All three took oysters Rockefeller from a slim Hispanic waiter.

Soon Lens and I arrived at the dark edge of the party. Waves pulsed against the cliffs below. The air was suddenly oceanic and unheated. We'd drifted outside the event and now turned to charge back through, back into the flimsy jazz.

Leo paused. He asked: Whom in there do you recognize?

There was the winner of the Bancroft Prize who had, as department chair, while drunk, felt up an untenured assistant professor. There was Blackface Metzger. Over there—I pointed at a pursy Englishman who had once been the Great Investigator of *The New Yorker*—he used force, didn't he? Hew says that guy should be in prison. And over there, of course, that's R. Kelly.

Yes, good, exactly. There are differences, said Leo. My pet hypothesis, to speak your language, is that these variations in past sins actually determine social clustering. The faculty are nearly all men, nearly all white, so this is how we've sorted ourselves into tribes.

It's almost Buddhist. You come here, are dipped in the river on the way, but something of your past remains.

Lens's eyes queried me. His writing often played at the margins of Eastern philosophy. Had I known this? Had I *intentionally* referred to one of his subjects?

My eyebrows responded: Yes.

Lens directed me from group to group and explained his taxonomy, the caste system he had identified. The highest status belonged to those like myself and Hew, who had come for ancillary personal reasons. We were sought after, for we alone had power to absolve, to forgive.

The next level down were those who had committed

only aesthetic offenses (this was Lens himself, he insisted) and who might well have stayed, however uncomfortably, on the mainland.

Then came those—the Institute's core constituency—who really did not have dignified options on the mainland. This broad category included those who gracefully accepted exile (Perry), those who were thought to be lucky not to be in prison, and those who had in fact been to prison but were out again.

At the very bottom—the lowest caste—were those who remained aggrieved, those who could not accept their sentences and hungered for opportunities to explain the *injustices* they had suffered, how they had been *right* all along. This group was the lowest caste not because zero injustices had occurred. Probably some had; no one in her right mind thought university administrators were actually infallible. But it was not good Institute style to long for the old world. The ethos was supposed to be: RIP to the old world, eyes front, we have a moon colony to build here.

Lens and I had monopolized each other for about an hour. I was building toward asking him something personal. I wanted to hear about Saul Bellow, who had once been Lens's champion, and about Kathleen Turner, whom he had almost married. In the crevices of Lens's face I glimpsed ruins of a lost culture, a life of analog Romanticism and glamour and solitude so outdated that no one I knew would tolerate it. Certainly Hew couldn't. But its appeal was visceral to me. Lens had been such a merciless artist—a danger to himself and others. He had betrayed his family with the book that made him famous, and after that had managed to betray everyone else whose betrayal might bring literary profit. He had lived as if true virtue meant to never be co-opted, to be understood only on one's own terms. It was impossible not to envy this. So I wanted more than he was giving me and was just about to ask what he was writing these days when he said: This was lovely, Helen. However, I am turning into a pumpkin.

Lens extended his hand, we shook, and he strode off, his slim shoulders disappearing into the dark.

Perry was nowhere. I could not imagine talking to anyone else, certainly not the octogenarian former news anchor now hobbling toward me. He was drooling, slightly, the cause of which might have been me or a more general infirmity. I darted through the party to the elevators, evading eye contact like an overtasked bartender.

In our apartment I ordered several books by Leo Lens to be brought from the library. They arrived in less than twenty minutes atop a robotic cart, under a silver cloche, like room service.

14.

The next day, Saturday, was the action in Philadelphia.

Someone had obtained a permit. Roads would be closed. Beyond this the organizing was disorganized, decentralized, gloriously and intentionally so. It was called An Action for Justice. Beyond justice you could bring your own priorities. Racial justice, economic justice, gender justice, religious justice, environmental justice, animal justice, and subgenres of each, all included and in slight mutual tension. The Action for Justice organically grew to a perverse size. Then cable news caught on. Between the day Hew decided to go and the day of the Action it had become hegemonic, an Important event, Woodstock. Wealthy socialists flew in from Portland and Berlin to take part.

Now it was debated, of course, whether some causes ought to bow to others. It was debated whether the message might *perhaps* be clearer if there were *fewer* messages? But what message ought to prevail? This of course could not be decided. There was no one authorized to decide such things. Not that it mattered. The Action was expressive, not persuasive. The world, all present would agree, was in chaos; it was regressing. The Action for Justice would be a great yowl.

Hew stayed with his high school friend, a chef, in a fifth-floor walk-up downtown. The building was a creaky holdout, structurally infirm and cluttered with outdated fixtures. It was destined soon for gut renovation that would, by historical conservation rules, expensively preserve its humdrum brick façade. The building's exterior already bore scaffolding papered with digital renderings of promised improvements.

Hew slept on the couch, and he had been lucky even to get a couch. Sleeping on the floor below him was a chef couple up from DC. They had arrived around 3 a.m., after finishing work at 1 a.m. Chefs were nuts generally but still this reflected the intense commitment this Action was eliciting. One chef slept on a thin camping mattress, the other on a yoga mat.

Hew woke to bustle. Through the open living room window, past the scaffolding, he saw hundreds of people passing the corner. It was 7:03 a.m. Once Hew was up, soon too were the DC chefs and Hew's friend. Another couple emerged from the guest bedroom in commando boots, flannels, gratuitous piercings. Everyone stood in the kitchen, blearily sipping coffee, introducing themselves. The others were *quite* interested to learn that Hew lived at RIP. But it was too early for that subject. For the first time in months Hew did not feel defensive; he was here; he had traveled to the Action for Justice.

So when a DC chef said: The Rubin Institute, man, what is *that* like?, Hew shrugged, said it sucked, did not get into it further. It was empowering to think of RIP as some ordinary backwater. Hew spoke not like a witness to a moral travesty but with the bummed resignation of someone who has been forced to move to Akron for work.

It emerged that the couple with the piercings were serious anarchists. Hew nodded coolly, implying that he was familiar with and had often before encountered militant anarchists, which was not so. They all went down into the crowd.

Hew texted me that he was Marching with anarchists!

I asked: Do you agree on anything?

He said: Justice.

The circular firing squad of chants eventually coalesced into a generic No Justice No Peace. Hew updated me on the getups: some dudes dressed like Mr. Monopoly, a Colonel Bernie Sanders distributing free fried chicken. There were gays embracing everyone, leaving unsolicited imprints of glitter and body paint. Hew had not had this much fun or this much humor about himself in many months. I had not liked him this much in many months. He seemed happy? Texting him, I felt Neptune knocking on the Seventh House and wished he were home — though of course if he had been home his mood would likely have required me to spend some additional time in lab.

They marched from Rittenhouse Square to the Liberty Bell, then south, then back west. The crowds overflowed all permitting. Downtown Philadelphia was a liquid of anger and solidarity. A fleet of drones swarmed overhead, collecting footage.

So it was very well documented when the Knights of Right entered the scene. Helpfully they had worn a distinct and flamboyant common palette, royal blue and vermilion, evoking Superman and their Übermensch mythology. All of this information per Hew, later. Eventually I watched some footage too. But as events unfolded in Philadelphia I was alternating my gaze between the dusky ocean and the third novel of Leo Lens. I had not had a day without both work and Hew in . . . two years? three? I was recalibrating. I was not keeping up with the news.

When Hew texted that he was okay, I did not understand why he would have been not-okay but nor did I think much of it. I responded: Glad it went well. Then I went back to reading.

A small counterprotest had attempted to stand its ground at Washington Square. Among the counterprotesters were various rightists: gun-lovers, abortion-haters, a small contingent of explicit white supremacists. They had their *own* permit. They had a *right* to stand where they stood. Predictably, though, they were overwhelmed. They were shoved around and pushed out, scattered, neutralized. The process had not been violent but it had not exactly been peaceful either. They felt mistreated. Probably they were mistreated. There was video, instantly viral with the Online Right, of a mob savagely berating a solitary middle-aged woman whose sign read Christ Loves All with a picture of a fetus. She just stood there and took it.

But the Knights of Right were not about to.

In their group chat, later produced in court, you could see how they conceived of their assault as an exfiltration. They had to get their people *out*. The Knights "mobilized," used SEAL lingo, wore MOPP 3, exchanged "sitreps," were "wheels up at 17:30." They also used SEAL equipment, pretty much.

Their Humvees plunged full bore into the crowd. The Knights carried AR-15s and tear gas, sported matching custom Kevlar vests. They decided they finally had just cause to massacre the very people they had always dreamed of massacring. In court the Knights argued "defense of another," a kind of *ideological* self-defense.

Hew witnessed it. He was never in immediate personal danger but he and the anarchists heard gunfire, screaming. They hid for a while behind the counter of a Starbucks. Then they ran for it. On the way home they saw blood on the pavement. Turning a corner, Hew tripped and fell and scraped his palms and fractured his thumb.

At the apartment they found the chefs—also okay. All embraced like family. They sat the rest of the night outside the apartment window, on top of the construction scaffolding, talking, smoking, keeping up with the coverage. Hew had never smoked before, or at least never an entire cigarette, but now he did. The Knights surrendered around midnight, once there was no one left to shoot besides cops, whom in general the Knights had nothing against. In total: twenty-nine dead, seventy-four critically injured. Sirens and police lights embraced the city until dawn.

It should have more seriously concerned me that Hew

was not talkative about his experience. Usually he was so discursive. He sorted ideas by airing them. He recounted the day to me but never expanded on the basics of what happened, the surface of his experience. I did not try to force his interior state out into the open. I was not sure I even had the ability to do this—or that it would behoove me to find out whether I did.

15.

With the simulation running, I had no pressing work. Fortuitous timing, for I was able to attempt to attend to Hew. I even cooked *for* Hew, without his help, which I almost never did. Without Hew's interventions and adjustments, without his intuition, I followed recipes as nervously as one might assemble a bomb—assuming the slightest variation would cause disaster. The few recipes I knew by heart all required meat except for a gazpacho where the sole preparation was to put the appropriate vegetables and spices in a blender. I had impressed Hew with my gazpacho the first time I cooked for him. Or maybe he had only pretended to be impressed. In any event it was relationship canon and carried fond associations. After he returned from Philly, I made the gazpacho in what I hoped would be a clear signal of tender feelings. I read more Lens with my feet propped against Hew's thigh. I wanted him to feel my attention, to feel that whenever he chose to open up about the Action I would be Present.

But he took his videoconferences, tweaked haywire database systems, and watched trashy medical TV all as usual. Or perhaps slightly more intently than usual. It was difficult to separate my own irking sense that something was unfinished—an open parenthesis, an ellipsis, a subroutine repeating ad infinitum—from whatever Hew might actually have been feeling. When I asked him directly to tell me how he was—to just, you know, *talk*—he said, What is there to talk about?

Trauma, maybe? You just underwent something. It must weigh on you; it would on anyone.

We were standing in the kitchen and Hew leaned over the counter, his arms braced against it like long lean pylons. He stared at the microwave. When introspective, he was not good at eye contact. He said, I don't really feel like it happened to me. I was nearby, but there were so many injured, so many killed, so many who lost friends and family. I think those were the people it happened to.

But *something* also happened to you. You're allowed to have feelings about this. You must have been terrified.

Yeah, I was scared for a few minutes. What else is there to say?

Aren't you angry?

I don't know—these things happen every few months. It's yet another time that some right-wing nutjobs decide to kill a bunch of people, and I don't know why I should be any angrier than I usually am. Just because this time I was there?

Well...yes.

Well...I'm not.

So while Hew went on being conspicuously normal, I explored. I ate lunch in the graduate dining room, sometimes even in the undergraduate dining hall, instead of ferrying my food back to lab. One day a professor of economics who had been wrong about affirmative action asked if I would like to lunch with him in the faculty dining room—purportedly an honor, plus it had a devastating dessert bar. Could he welcome me to the Institute? I demurred. But I was not bothered to be asked. Nor for a while was I bothered by the others who approached me— in the dining halls, in the atrium, on the paths around campus, in the cafés in town. I felt the way I imagined the popular girls had felt in high school: everyone was so friendly! Suddenly I had broad appeal. This was new for me—I'd always been too young for my grade, too head-down and cerebral to provoke much interest—and I'll admit I enjoyed it. Determining how to evade these invitations was a quick social puzzle. The constraint I set for myself was that I could not be generic. I could be truthful but only if the truth would be vaguely offensive, along the lines of: No, *thank* you, though, I am going to go walk around alone.

Which I in fact did. While the simulation ran, I walked the island in my yellow windbreaker. I played tourist. I went down along the blustery beaches, atop the cliffs, through the clusters of pristine Cape Cod houses. In town I ate almond croissants, drank espresso, and watched boats patiently keen in the wharf. The island had a forest of petite coastal pines. In the sandy island soil, nothing too tall remained for long. I meandered through the forest trails, up to rocky points—their views mostly ruined by the Endowment—and listened to the wind and surf. I felt nature around me. In theory all I did for a living was study the natural world, but what I studied was pretty much that: nature in theory, too abstract and small and intense to be experienced. Now I was accessing nature phenomenologically, catching glimpses of the sublime.

What was I looking for with all this wandering? Leo Lens, of course. Though I could not quite admit this to myself. I was walking around, and between walks I was reading up—reading Lens and about Lens.

But *intellectual* interest was not *interest*, was it?

Anyway I was not going to ask Perry where Lens lived. My hope was for an organic experience. I wished simply, and in various senses of the word, to encounter him.

16.

I had apparently absorbed from Dad a lot of Leo Lens's history, and accordingly my investigation of him, which I was determined to do systematically, progressed swiftly.

In the beginning, Leopold Lens had seemed a loyal-enough disciple. His first book took up the prosaic frustrations and virtuous intentions of a family rather unlike his own (goyish, unmonied). The novel ended elegiacally; an uncaring world would not let these fine, salt-of-the-earth people catch a break. In other words, it was a mediocre and conventionally moral book that sold well and received praise. Even Dad did not love this one, and I determined to skip it, for I understood the most interesting thing about that first book to be how Lens had reacted to its popularity.

Some people will succeed and, having succeeded, repeat the steps that generated success. Others will succeed and, having succeeded, choose never to succeed in that particular way again.

Lens was twenty-three at this point. His parents were proud; they had made a *real writer*. He gave talks and sold books at synagogues all over Long Island, Queens, Brooklyn. The Jews of Long Island were proud. *They* had made a real writer. But Lens went to Chicago, where he and Saul Bellow drank scotch at the Quad Club under the pretext of a literary interview. Lens's publisher had sent the book, for blurbs, to Bellow and Nabokov and Joseph Heller. Nabokov and Heller said nil. Bellow took the time to write back that he could not blurb the book because it was not very good. Accordingly Lens now expected Bellow to give it to him straight.

Bellow asked, Are you a *kind* person?

Lens said, I try to be.

Why?

Lens had been raised right, so he could think of many reasons to be kind, but immediately he knew that writing well was not one of them.

Do my books seem *un*kind, to you? said Bellow.

The minute attention you pay to people; that is love, that is affection, isn't it?

Bellow shrugged. Call it what you like. The point is that my family that I've been writing about—it's over, dead, and I killed it. I put the whole procedure of our life in plain air.

I see, said Lens. He liked his family. He liked Jews. They had all been kind to him. And for his next book he sautéed and seared and diced them, presenting the world with his first delectable creation. Of course his mother, father, sister, aunts, synagogue, felt abused, to put it mildly. Lens's position—in an interview he claimed he actually said this to his mother—was: You are meat. I will slaughter and serve and smoke and roast you, in perpetuity. I am cooking for a world of carnivores.

By the time Lens was thirty, his family no longer spoke to him or, really, to one another.

But now he had Bellow. He had a guild committed to his same project, to place everything ugly in the open, to put *life* right on the page, to write truthfully if not factually about living people. Lens: unusually merciless. He had Joyce and Mary McCarthy and Henry Roth in the background; he had Babel and Bellow. Lens felt the proverbial torch in his hand as he became another dot, another dash, in a great tradition. For a few years he and Bellow could be seen with some regularity drinking scotch at the Quad Club.

But it soon turned out that Lens had, perhaps, not learned quite what Bellow intended to teach him. Bellow had probably meant something like: kindness typically requires sentimentality and cliché, so you will not be honest while you are trying to be kind, while you are trying to *be* anything.

What Lens made from this was: Propriety, tradition, attachment, are death for art.

Nothing Lens wrote about Bellow could have angered Bellow. What betrayed Bellow was his abandoning realism to write a *language* novel. It was postmodern, playful, abstract, spare. For another writer, an outsider, sure, this could be an acceptable style. But for Lens, who had been emerging as a new master of social realism, to jump into philosophical novelizing, into language writing—it was a repudiation. It was Dylan going electric. It declared that Lens believed that anything Bellow wrote for the rest of his life would be aesthetically antiquated, dead on arrival.

It was all the worse a betrayal that Lens's audience now grew. Critics proclaimed that Lens had matured. Scholars decided Lens was worth theorizing. Even as Lens moved into Kathleen Turner's house in Malibu—and out again two months later—he perpetuated the notion of his own seriousness by publishing progressively less-readable fiction. Soon his referents shifted from Hollywood to academia obscura: a pastiche of stolen passages from out-of-print Americana, quotes from the diaries of Grigory Orlov, footnotes in baseball history, the Abhidhamma Piṭaka, Virgil, deep Talmud. It was catnip for people like Dad, and of course for the critics and professors. This era of Lens's writing promised that there would always be more juice if you kept squeezing.

But when I tried to read it, I wondered: Had he been *attempting* to lose his audience? I had the sense, from his work in these difficult years, that he loathed anyone who would take the time to understand him. And Lens did finally betray his fans and critics—and in particular Farrar, Straus and Giroux—by declining to publish anything for eleven years. He went to the Catskills to teach. He sold the Manhattan apartment his second advance had bought him. And in his absence some unfavorable opinions calcified— that Lens was no more than a fine stylist; that his most conventional, autobiographical work was his best; that the rest was as misguided as *Finnegans Wake*. Only the scholars—

vested interests—and true devotees—like my dad—were hanging in there, certain that Lens had more to give.

There were women, always women, but for him women were episodes. One could see in his work how deeply he longed for someone to stick—and how no one did—and how his characters grew jaded about their own hearts. He had no known engagements after Kathleen Turner. Probably he was too jealous of his time, of interruption, for domesticity. Indeed he was soon known at his university as a bad professional citizen; he had insisted on a provision in his contract that would exempt him from even the monthly departmental meeting.

He reserved all spare attention for his students, who for the most part did not want it. Lens could be as ruthless with student work as he was with his own; moreover, it was understood that Lens, alone among the faculty, would not help you secure an agent or publisher. The idea, as Lens infamously proclaimed at the beginning of each workshop, was: Other people can help you charm the gatekeepers. I intend to help you write something worth reading. Typically only rather self-serious men were enticed by this offer, since typically, by this point, only rather self-serious men thought that Lens himself was worth reading. Lens outwardly appeared to be estranging himself from the world. He was not publishing, was a disengaged colleague, remained unmarried and had no children. Was he even writing, or did he plan to coast for the rest of his life on tenure and dwindling royalties?

Every day around 5 p.m., when he did not have company, Lens became promiscuous. He made phone calls. He'd stay on the line for hours, mostly with other writers, with musicians and mathematicians. For three or four hours every night, he gossiped and argued and joked, pacing around his living room in a telemarketer's headset. He'd gotten this tendency from his mother, he later told me. His friends said he would call without warning and then not let you off the phone for two hours; you would have this moment of wanting to screen the call, but inevitably you'd pick up. Conversing with him could be as rich as literature. You ended up confessing things about yourself that you had never previously realized.

And before 5 p.m., Lens did his job. His next book was, for Dad and his ilk, vindication. Not a long novel, actually, despite eleven years in the works. But it had the distinct feel of an iceberg, every word on the page ballasted by an enormous subsurface mass. Lens had invented a new alter ego and a new voice for himself. Where his earlier work had toggled between different registers, almost different languages, Lens's voice in *Juvenilia* was at ease, integrated. It reminded me of the way he moved. He had spent a decade honing this book's voice. Really he'd been honing himself, dispensing with what he did not need.

In other words, I thought, hadn't he been doing the same thing I did for a living—finding the most elegant means to capture and distill complexity? He had become a numericist of his own life.

Juvenilia—its final chapters remain among my most intense experiences of art. When I closed the book, I felt like a cracked egg. I wanted to call Dad, but he believed I had already read *Juvenilia* years before. I badly wanted to find Lens. It was a blustery, dark day. I grabbed my wind-breaker and went for the door with such urgency that Hew asked if I was mad at him.

Over the next five years, Lens produced a series of short novels, grounded by the same narrator, that were thought by his loyal but diminished audience to be art and craft of the highest sort. I devoured all five in two days.

Nonetheless. There was literature, and then there was life. His late-life productivity did not convert into currency with the new department chair or the new dean of the faculty. He was considered vestigial; ideologically he was loathed. Historically Lens's absenteeism had been sufficient to maintain the peace, but suddenly they had to *deal* with him, because one day he had been goaded into saying:

All right, you would like examples? Cynthia Ozick, whom I consider one of the only living masters, queen and heir to the glittering world of literature. George Eliot, whom I do not even try to imitate. Virginia Woolf, whom I have never stopped studying, even though she would have thought I was a gross, grubby Jew. So there are a great number of writers who happen to be women whom I admire. None of them, alas, happen to be students in this class.

(When I found out about this, I wanted to smack Lens across the face. Can't you see, I said, that if you are going to advocate for such enormous liberty, such a wide aperture for art and free speech and academic discretion, you really have to watch your mouth? Why *is* it, do you think, that all of you who are so righteously resisting the so-called thought police turn out to be bullies?)

After this incident—and after the dean determined that Lens could not be fired over it—Lens was not merely unpopular, he was *persona non*. As a student you could not elect to take his courses without your choice hanging over you, forcing you to spend party after party playing the apologist, justifying baby vs. bathwater. It was a lot of bother to work with a guy who was not even going to help your career, so one semester literally zero students did. All of which made Lens's salary, anchored in the years when he had been the headliner among the faculty, all the more irksome to the department. For what Lens presently cost, they could hire 3.6 socially acceptable adjuncts who might actually lighten others' teaching loads.

The weather got pretty cold. Soon it was thought to be his moral obligation to quit, abandon tenure, thereby freeing the department from its budgetary crisis.

Now, one might think that Lens, having betrayed and moved beyond his family, Judaism, popularity, critics, Saul Bellow, Kathleen Turner, would be indifferent to all of this. He did try to give that appearance in the plodding calm with which he taught his not-even-a-handful of students. But his work was all rage and glee, smirking disappointment and exasperated futility. He drew, in one book, a strikingly extended analogy between a certain Catskills university and the People's Commissariat for Internal Affairs. He was as learned and livid and energetic as he had ever been, but it would not be right to say Lens was enjoying himself. It was like being strapped to a moving car. He could not catch his breath, plus he was getting older...

Then came B.W. Rubin's offer to come, live, write, *don't teach,* you will *never talk to an administrator again for the rest of your life*—this was not, as he'd told me, something Lens could pass up.

Perhaps he thought he could evolve one last time? That was something I surmised during the rather large amount of time I was spending wandering, reading, and surmising about Leo Lens.

17.

Then the simulation finished.

It would be 6:13 a.m. give or take a few minutes when it stopped running. Perry and I met in lab at 6:15. I had slipped from bed in the cool fall dark, pulled on leggings and a sweatshirt, and now clutched my coffee with brittle fingers. Perry was in his version of casual dress, which meant all the fixings minus tie.

We sat silently at our terminals, scrolling. The first thing was to check landmarks, to see whether the model had accurately simulated known experimental data. Then we would see whether the rest of the results, which had no experimentally determined targets, were remotely coherent.

For twenty or maybe thirty minutes, we did not talk. Occasionally Perry grunted or I sighed.

Something was way off.

Truly it was nonsense. We had expected a useful failure but this was not that. It was like a monkey had written our code.

The atoms of any given material fit together in a kind of lattice, and our model, like most HTS models, showed how electrical current caused electrons to move through various lattices. The results can be presented as a kind of heat map, showing density of electrons at a particular location. In general it should look pretty even, continuous—you should see flow and lanes. What we had was the equivalent of a blizzard in Phoenix while it's 120 degrees in Tucson while at the same time in Albuquerque there is a null set, simply no weather at all. Certain obvious differences in conditions and materials had been bleached away. The most rational piece of the results suggested that nearly every substance on Earth—including, like, granite and wood—would superconduct at 97°C. This was extremely untrue.

I died a little, seeing it. Humans are not built to fail this badly this early in the morning. For months I had been so optimistic, had felt so *productive*. I'd thought the move to RIP was already paying off. Perry and I had developed bold hypotheses and an innovative structure that would allow us, we thought, to run simulations in one-fifth the time that would advance the ball five times faster than our peers. The new physical ideas were all Perry's, but figuring out how to represent and combine them had been all me—and I really thought we'd made a breakthrough, that I'd done some of my cleverest math yet.

Perry did not say much. Many people met him and thought it must all come so naturally. Perry seemed, if you were not paying close attention, to be such a dandy, such a hedonist, so *casually* brilliant. He was a gossip; he gabbed and gladhanded; he did not seem like someone who *worked*. But he was. No one lucks into a Nobel Prize at thirty-eight. He had drive. It was never more visible than when he had been disappointed.

Perry stood, hands lodged in pockets, and—speaking for the first time in ten minutes—said: Let's regroup tomorrow.

I stayed in lab alone for another few hours, transfixed by our disaster.

18.

Leopold Lens's breakthrough story, published in the *Paris Review,* was "A Snug Business," a then-modern adaptation of "Bartleby the Scrivener." Already by the time I read it the thing was hysterically out of date. The world it depicted was closer to Melville's than to mine; business still happened on paper. In Lens's version, the scrivener character took on the role of Melville's narrator: an attorney, though one of the lower ranks. After a period of unemployment, Lens's Bartleby—called only L, in the abstract literary fashion of that era—is hired by one of New York's white-shoe legal behemoths. He is the firm's sole Jew. He is not partner-track. At first he works and works and works. There are towers of boxes in the client's storage room. He is ravenous for documents. He devours these boxes, processing, filing, and tagging with such focus and for such long hours that the other storage-room attorneys grow resentful.

L hears them discussing his "Jewish ambition." Does he really think a Jew can *sweat* his way into the partnership? L is unflapped, unstoppable.

Do you not see, they coax L, that even our employers wish us to work *slower*? This because the firm is paid hourly, so time is profit.

Still L devours.

Until he stops. Bartleby said "I would prefer not to." L says "Yeah, I don't think so." Suddenly he will do no more than stare at whatever is placed in front of him. His increasingly agitated supervisor and coworkers prod him. He is given every incentive, every opportunity. But it is as if he has eaten all he can for the rest of his life. He will not quit, will not leave the premises, and will not work either. He sits all day at his desk, staring.

They do not fire him. Firing the firm's first and sole Jew would not send the right message in a changing world. Also, the main thing is that L's time remains billable. Indeed he continues to be their most profitable reviewer. He is always at the office. He stares *at the documents*—this much is undeniable—and accordingly, the firm's executive committee decides, his time may be billed to clients within the ethics of the profession. Clients of course could not know to complain. L's time is a rounding error. So it all continues.

This story was deemed a penetrating commentary on white-collar work, professional ethics, and the role of the Jew in the fracturing gentility of post–Nixon America.

Maybe L inspired me, granted me some kind of permission. I read the story in bed, where I had retreated the afternoon of the model's failure. For a while after that I was L; I was Bartleby. For weeks I had devoured our problem, had worked and worked and worked. Now I was distracted and demoralized. In high-def hindsight I could see every misstep we'd made, and it was Perry, I felt, who had led us down the wrong path. His instructions were to blame. His bullying will, his egomaniacal insistence that we ought to cram our model with every passing idea Perry Fucking Smoot had ever had—that was the problem. My code implementing his will had been meticulous, mostly.

Perry did not exactly blame me but would not admit his errors either. It was maddening. Instead he was all about new ideas, moving on. He thought we could kowtow to HTS modeling convention a little more, maybe, but only with some onerous and in his view insightful modifications. His energy was exhausting. I didn't have any patience for it right then. I went to lab but remained so stewed that I could not really work. I sat at my terminal reading Lens or watching British gardening shows on my desktop, with our code open and dormant in the adjacent window. British horticulture was very soothing and contained just enough science to hold my attention.

I read Lens and took long walks as if I still had nothing to do. Soon I had covered every winding pine trail and every curling muffled lane on the island. Lens remained elusive. Once, I thought I saw him enter the Endowment. But by the time I reached the atrium he had vanished, and instead I was greeted by a reedy, pimpled international relations doctoral student who had already twice failed to grasp that we were not allies.

The shine of it-girl status pretty quickly wore off. I was already struggling with unusual distractibility, and I had always been a think-while-walking type. But now every time I paced around campus, seeking focus, and felt I might just *finally* be getting some momentum on a worthwhile train of thought...there would be a man around every corner, it seemed, eager to interrupt me. A confident hand or brazen invitation was extended. Several different men, puzzlingly, asked me if I'd like to join them for a game of backgammon, the erotic potential of which I did not find obvious.

Other men, and perhaps this was naïve of me, seemed less interested in a sexual encounter than in moral affirmation. They wanted some sign that a young woman like myself would converse with contemptible creatures like them. Several men played the sensitive ally, their hands reaching out to cup my shoulder: *How* are you holding up here? Can't be easy. And after Philadelphia? So horrible...are you all right? Yet other men drafted some professional pretext along the lines of: I am *so intrigued* by your work on high-temperature superconductivity. It might indeed be relevant to my own work on XYZ, which of course it wasn't. This one historian, a Frenchman who had harassed at least twenty of his graduate students before his university caught up with him, seemed to get a little troll thrill from greeting me, and surely plenty of other women, with a "*Bonjour,* beautiful" every time we crossed paths. He was flaunting his liberty, daring us to try reporting him when there was no one to whom to report such things.

The attention was crazy-making and also a complete bore. I would say I was married, was on my way somewhere urgently, was weaving a burial shroud and could not *possibly* consider any new appointments until this important duty was done. With bolder fellows I was emboldened myself: I let myself be as big a cunt as I could without creating an incident. I wanted to grab some of these guys by the lapels and shout: Can't you see yourself? Can't you see that you would have *no interest in me whatsoever* in the real world? Nevertheless they persisted. I tried to think what I could have done to prevent myself from becoming such a target. I had somehow stayed below male radar for the first two months of term, but no longer. Some men, like the international relations guy, were plainly on the lookout for me. I thought maybe I shouldn't have worn that dress to the Lucretius Festival, shouldn't have been seen with Lens? Had my appearance, just one time, as a faintly sexual object—and the subsequent revanishing of that object beneath my sweatshirts, parkas, greasy hair, and crazed temperament—incited a quest among the Institute's men to turn me out once and for all?

With Hew, I had to downplay how irritating it was. For one thing I felt stupid whining to Hew post-Philly. The other reason, probably salient, was that I did not want to arm my own rebels. I expected Hew to use these advances like ammunition in his campaign to get us to move literally anywhere else—and at this point I still wanted to stay and keep working. Despite current conditions, Perry remained my only real shot at solving HTS. Perry and I still almost *expected* we would do it. This felt increasingly like an insane expectation, one I wished to be free of, but nonetheless, there it was.

And nonetheless, I had, for weeks, been unable to let go of the model as it had been. I was aggrieved and sentimental about it. Any moment, I thought, some tweak would occur to me and every other piece would fall into its right place and all would be well. So I had been fiddling at the edges: copying and pasting, editing, restructuring. It was a colorable simulation of work. What I could not seem to do was write anything *new*.

One day we were in Perry's office. Perry sat behind his desk, his huge window behind him, and behind that the afternoon sunlight glared off the sea. As we wrapped up, my laptop folded dormant on my knees, Perry's posture became erect. Suspiciously professional.

He said, Let's discuss a schedule.

A schedule?

The new draft of the model. I'd like us to have a time-line. We can break the work into stages.

Okay—but—to what end?

I would like us to accelerate our process.

You mean my process.

We've stalled lately. It's understandable—but enough's enough. I've listed a number of projects, modules we know we must write for the next iteration, and some dates by which drafts of those modules ought to be ready for my review. Of course there are open questions too, and we will decide those and adjust as we go, but in the meantime there is no reason to continue dawdling about the work we know we must do regardless.

Perry slid a sheet of paper across his desk—he had actually printed it—conveying a table of tasks and dates. Deadlines. This was a first. He was treating me like other people, like an employee.

Afterward I rode down to the seventeenth floor, fuming. Hew was in the midst of some crisis of backup servers. Until his call ended, I clanked around the kitchen, pretending to bake. I had no understanding of whatever issue Hew was managing, but his phone call endured a lot longer than seemed reasonable, so by the time he disconnected I was pretty pissed at him too.

Darling, he said. What are you doing? His eyebrows hovered way above his glasses, tolerant, amused. He surveyed my scatter of bowls and sieves.

It's nothing, I said.

Sometimes we felt like a closed thermodynamic system: a finite amount of strength between the two of us, and one of us could not lose some without it flowing to the other. For a few weeks I had been trying to tend to Hew, but now Hew took command. He stood, tucked his rolling chair beneath the desk, and folded into a lanky stretch. I continued clattering. His head between his legs, he said, Please— the bowls—relent. Are you trying to bake something?

I *will* bake something. A cake. Or bread.

Has someone clubbed you on the head?

Figuratively, yes.

Let's walk it off. The atmosphere in here, this building, it's poison.

We went along the cliffs. We hiked out to the high point on the island, from which you could see its entirety.

Can I just say—

No, Hew said. You can complain on the way back. For now, just look.

Endowment aside, maybe even with the Endowment, it was beautiful, this island like a little village on a cookie that had been cut out of New England. Hew's finger drew loops on the small of my back, and we inhaled cold salty air.

We walked back in the dark—our narrow, dimly lit path juxtaposed against the wide dark winter sea. We could feel the water more than we could see it.

Okay, Hew said, go for it.

So what he doesn't realize, I said re Perry, is that I am *spent*. Everything that I had in the tank, I put into the version of our model that just failed. He thinks he can force me to sit down and solve problems that even *he* cannot solve? It's ridiculous, and unrealistic, and frankly disrespectful, after five years. Like what has he been doing for two decades? Now he's setting *deadlines*?? What I am doing right now—*this is the process*. We need a *very* big change. We need to completely reconceptualize our approach. It is not going to happen with incrementalism or brute force. Every genuinely good idea I've ever had has stewed for weeks or months while I apparently do nothing about it. I mean *that* is what I'm doing right now. I think. Maybe it looks, even feels to me, like I am screwing around. But things are stewing, you know? And if I already *knew* what was stewing I would not need to *keep* stewing. The point being that it's not like I can give him *status* updates. The *point* being *fuck him*.

Nothing would have improved Hew's life more, and more immediately, than a permanent rupture between me and Perry. So it was really commendable that he did not drive the wedge. When I had finished all my fury and justification, Hew grasped my shoulders and said: Oh, my delicate genius.

This was a term he used to signify that I was above my usual quotient of diva.

Well, *kinda*? I said.

Yeah, I mean, I know, sweetie.

Maybe I'll try Mandarin again.

We went home. As we shed our coats, I said: Maybe I'm just humiliated. It turned out so badly—even with Perry's stupid task list, I don't know where to begin fixing it. I couldn't tell you the last time I was this confused. I have been looking at the model, this huge complicated thing that I built—I mean this is my *child*—and I just *do not care*.

So maybe Perry is onto something? suggested Hew. Maybe all you can do is get your butt back in the chair.

Unlike me, Hew managed a team and understood professional coercion, the currencies with which those who lacked self-motivation were nonetheless prodded to work.

Yeah, of course he is, I said. Therefore fuck him. Let's watch some TV.

19.

It helped to realize that Perry had no recourse, really, if I ignored his instructions. He couldn't fire me: I was his motor. Without me he would be in a dinghy with only one oar. One trend among physicists is that seniority brings resistance to writing your own code. In part this is justified because programming best practices do evolve; in part this is the vanity of wanting to be the big-ideas guy. Perry was more hands-on than most but still there was a lot of detail work he opposed doing himself and did not trust anyone but me to do for him. Once I reminded myself of this, I did not feel so coerced by his deadlines and met many of them voluntarily, regarding which Perry probably thought himself a master of motivational technique...

But whatever. Not all worthwhile creation occurs in an inspired thrall. It helps to simply proceed, to measure progress quantitatively: lines of code, subroutines "completed," however half-assed and ham-handed. There was something freeing, too, about working the model like a nine-to-five. I left it at lab. I read and I took my walks. I stood alone in the woods watching my steamy breath bloom, feeling like no more or less than a human being. Hew and I somehow had sex three times (!!!) in one week. These did not have the mechanical feel to which we'd grown accustomed. I was open and Hew was urgent, a little violent, clutching my throat, pressing me down. Usually I had to get him drunk before he'd do that.

There was something new going on for both of us.

What I *thought* was going on with Hew was that maybe his near-death experience at the Action had reinvigorated him. His new mood was too intense to be called *joie de vivre,* but certainly he was in keener spirits than he'd been in since we moved to the Institute.

What I thought was going on with me was that for once I was not consumed by work and was, simultaneously, crushing pretty hard on Leo Lens. I felt avid, libidinal. Hew, the appropriate outlet, was not inclined to inquire into the cause of the recent improvements in our physical relations. I was not inclined to examine the Freudian resonance of turning on for a guy who was, in age and spirit, my dad.

20.

Every now and then B.W. permitted protesters to come to the Institute itself, instead of shouting at it from afar. This enabled Institute students, faculty, and staff to join the protests without a commute, which demonstrated open-mindedness and that the Institute did not fear but rather welcomed dissent—provided the dissenters were not a permanent annoyance to the serious work everyone was supposedly doing. Additionally, B.W. enjoyed gazing down at demonstrators from his penthouse. Sometimes he threw parties, so that others could sip cocktails and gaze down with him.

The inciting cause of the Thanksgiving RIP protest and the Thanksgiving RIP party were the same. The Institute had beaten its case.

There were in fact two cases—legal challenges on which the Institute's future rested—decided within a week of each other. The first was an attempt to invoke Title IX to attack the Institute's egregious gender inequities, the argument being that a woman would not have the same educational opportunities at the Institute as a man unless additional antiharassment rules were imposed. A plausible claim, but the Institute did not take federal money; Title IX did not apply; case dismissed.

The other case was the Institute's own successful challenge to Connecticut's attempts to regulate it out of existence. Under ever-mounting political pressure, the state had imposed a series of property taxes, operations taxes, and occupancy taxes that would, without expressly saying so, apply only to the Institute. The language by which the state accomplished this was inelegant: "Any privately owned institute of education or scholarship, located upon a body of land surrounded entirely by water, not more than 45 nautical miles from the City of New Haven, shall..." The state had further passed a law requiring any "institution of higher learning" to implement an administrative process to "fairly adjudicate" complaints involving racial bias and sexual misconduct according to specifically enumerated procedural requirements. RIP was, of course, the only qualifying institution in the state that did not already have such procedures. State legislators openly stated their intent to run B.W. out of town. The courts struck down these highly targeted laws for discriminating against the Institute's political viewpoint, in violation of the First Amendment.

All of which was taken as yet more infuriating evidence that the very rich were above the rules in our country. B.W. had bought himself a fiefdom. He was a colonizer. Actually he was—this analogy became popular—an *awful* lot like the Pilgrims. He had come bearing gifts and money, and made the native society an offer it thought it wanted. They had welcomed him, given him permits to build on historic Plymouth Island. But now, well—had he *stolen their land*? Technically he'd paid but it was starting to look like the indigenous liberal puritans of New England had gotten a raw deal—and like there was now nothing they could do, legally speaking, to unwind it.

Thus the Thanksgiving RIP demonstration and B.W.'s concurrent party.

The press could not resist the standoff. Camera crews interviewed protesters on the ferry over. Drones and helicopters swarmed the coast. The money shot—B.W. gave it to them—was the chanting outraged masses, zoom out, pan up along phallic tower, zoom in on penthouse window, there: a tuxedoed megabillionaire, fondling scotch, looking down, not *quite* smirking.

Hew and I parted ways that day. Naturally he went to the protest. Unexpectedly we had also been invited to B.W.'s soirée, which was otherwise mostly for tenured faculty. A card slipped under our door. Our Presence would be Warmly Received on the 42nd Floor at 5 o'clock for Festivities marking the Thanksgiving Season and Our Institute's recent Successes in Court.

The idea that Hew would attend was laughable. We fought because he thought the idea that *I* would go should be similarly laughable, while I in fact wanted to.

Hew kept cleaning his glasses—one of his stress signifiers. He said: Compromising, corrupting, you cannot drink their champagne without being at least a little bit *with* them. If you are not coming with me at least for god's sake *stay home.*

I heard the plea in his voice but still I said: This is the Endowment Penthouse! You can see Yale through a telescope! Who knows whether that invitation ever comes again. It will be an *experience.* I'm not so insecure that I think my values will be *compromised* just by attending a party whose host I disagree with.

We were both being pretty mean.

I was also being dishonest. The first and last time I'd seen Lens, there was a party. Perhaps parties were what caused him to emerge? If there was any party Leo Lens would want to attend, I was sure it was this one.

Hew stormed out. I dressed up.

Pressing 42-PH in the elevator, I felt a chill, like I was launching into the stratosphere. My hair was perfect. My dress was not especially revealing but was, in context, a provocation. If I was already an object of interest to all these men, I thought, I might as well interest the right man. I wanted Lens to want to *claim* me.

The elevator slid open onto a marble antechamber. Some pedestals held ancient statuary, Roman, surely (astonishingly) authentic. They were reverently lit, highlighted against the matte marbled walls. Between the artifacts stood women with ballet-dancer proportions who would check your coat and supply you with wine or Perrier.

No ordinary word for a human dwelling did this place justice. Technically we might call it an apartment, a condo, a residence. "Palace" more accurately communicates the feel, but even this omits the sense you had, so high above the island that you could not see ground without looking almost straight down from the long curving windows, of *hovering* above the sea.

Anyway the apartment was in maddeningly good taste. Hew and I liked to imagine that wealth was wasted on the wealthy, that once you had too much money you became destined to burn it on gauche extravagance, that you must run out of good ideas but still have so much money that you started purchasing many bad ideas, littering your life with them. Many rich people in fact do this. Not B.W., however. He possessed, or had hired, exceptional taste. The décor was a thrilling eclectic clutter of modern and classical paintings, ancient statuary of Europe and the Far East, antique clocks, armillary spheres, layered rugs of complementary textures, Persian carvings, modern and classical furniture, ornate wood cupboards— all made improbably cohesive. There was a tall red-scale Rothko above—in fact slightly occluded by—a large iron sewing table, on which sat an ancient Greek marble foot, an early American woodprint of a howling dog, a white-wicker-and-sea-glass vase of dried chrysanthemum, and a pair of exquisite Japanese cricket cages. One would not expect these things to go together but after a glance one could not imagine them arranged any other way, like *of course* one should place a sewing table directly in front of a Rothko.

This place induced overwhelming envy. I think I am less interested in object acquisition than most people of my time and class, male or female. But still—it was among the first times I thought it might be worthwhile to try J.P. Morgan. Even years later I still think about those cricket cages on the sewing table—and on the other side of the room a van Gogh embedded in a wall of Chinese watercolor scrolls, the harmonious contrast between them a genius feat of curating. This was the kind of thing I had opinions about because when I was a kid Dad had gone through a fine art phrase, dragging Mom and me, and later just me, to the Smithsonian and the National Gallery and the Philadelphia Museum of Art every few months.

The party was, by the standards of the Institute, fairly standard and noninflammatory. B.W. was playing the event straight: lite chamber music, staff in ordinary starched shirts, gorgeous New American hors d'ocuvres, most of which I could not eat. Pissed as I was with Hew, much as I was *over* him at that particular moment and would have enjoyed a spiteful beef tartare, my veganism felt like a firm contractual commitment. It was settled, at least while we remained at the Institute.

For a while I wandered around, so immersed in ogling the décor that I did not much notice, or at least was not much bothered by, any eyes ogling me.

Eventually I found Perry. We were not in the state of brain-meld we sometimes achieved but relations were on the mend. We had decided to make the model bulkier and more conventional. So for a few weeks I'd been learning Fortran, a prehistoric programming language I had never before needed but which was exceptionally efficient at certain kinds of matrix multiplication, the exceptional efficiency of which would minimize the run time of a bad bottleneck, a nineteen-line subroutine that had to repeat several million times before the rest of the model could progress. All of which is to say that Perry understood I was doing some very unglamorous work and he knew that revising the model would take me a while.

None of this appeared to be on Perry's mind. He held court beside a medieval tapestry of a unicorn under attack, valiantly defending itself from a mob of French hunters and dogs. I was quite sure I understood whom B.W. identified with in this image—and that Dad and I had once seen this exact tapestry exhibited at the Cloisters.

Beside Perry, within his wingspan, stood an extremely handsome boy. He was probably "of age" but it would not be accurate to call him a man.

I thought: This is news.

Perry's gestures and posture indicated ownership, pride, like the boy was another Nobel Prize. The boy looked pleased with his situation, like he thought *Perry* was the trophy.

Helen! Perry boomed.

He introduced me as his best student, which of course I was, but the whole thing felt performative given where Perry and I were with each other. I did not know the others standing in Perry's orbit, except for Dr. Markus Hellman-Combs, an immunologist who had been fired as editor of the *New England Journal of Medicine* for refusing to fire an assistant editor who had said online that the causal connection between structural racism and poor health outcomes had not yet been conclusively established. I knew the doctor because he had come up to me once in the Endowment lobby, introduced himself as an acquaintance of Perry's, and shortly thereafter had asked if I was available for a drink, perhaps he could cure what ailed me, har har.

Presently the doctor stood beside his wife and did not seem ashamed at introducing us.

Last came the introduction I was waiting for. This is Williams, said Perry.

William, nice to meet you, I said.

William*s*, Perry clarified. It was his parents' *alma mater*— and mine, in fact!

Williams, it emerged, was an undergraduate concentrating in linguistics. He was considering a PhD. In high school he had been a regionally ranked swimmer, his best stroke the butterfly. All of this information Perry disclosed on Williams's behalf.

They seemed, could it be, *coupled*? I was jarred. I had never seen Perry and Devlin together; I realized I had never seen Perry with *anyone*. He had always seemed to me a kind of a brain in a vat, a brilliant sexless entity, a Pokémon whose power was theoretical physics. Obviously he was gay, but this had previously seemed like more of a personality than an actual sexual drive. Suddenly I sensed the presence of active male equipment.

I excused myself to find B.W.'s Yale telescope.

It's delightful, said Perry. At night the Beinecke Library just *shines*.

Meandering through the party, I was now attuned to a different kind of décor. B.W. flaunted perhaps three-hundred million dollars in art and antiques. The faculty flaunted the sexually available students that B.W. had, indirectly, procured for them. The Perry-Williams pairing was par. And I was, it seemed, one of the few women not attending as a faculty +1. I jostled past a former Harvard Law School dean, who stood in a conservative suit, with conspicuous dignity and reserve, beside a conspicuously pert undergraduate.

21.

The study was not off-limits but was empty when I entered. Heavy bookcases led the eye past leather couches to a vast mahogany desk, a sculptural lamp, a modest task chair, and—at the picture window, facing northwest—a telescope. It occurred to me that the entire Endowment had been calculated around this view. The room was architecturally overdetermined. The building's position on the island, and this room's precise height above the sea, enabled B.W. to see over the curvature of the earth, through New Haven harbor, to Yale. You could not see the mainland at all from the lower floors— the floors occupied by housing, offices, classrooms. Only B.W.'s domain possessed this visual link to what once was.

The telescope's settings and position were locked, its tripod bolted to the floor. As I said: overdetermined. A small engraved panel announced the telescope's sole use: to examine "Yale, the past." Both technically true.

The telescope showed Yale as it had been a subsecond earlier—the time required for light to refract off those neo-Gothic spires and travel forty miles to the telescope to your eye. Aim this telescope upward and it could see back a few hundred thousand years, at starlight only just arriving. The fixation of the telescope upon Yale, the insistence that it was *the past,* pertained to B.W.'s bitter expulsion from the board of the Yale Corporation. Before founding the Institute, he had intended, with the enticement of $1.3 billion, to reshape Yale's culture and save it from itself. Yale, however, had not wanted to be saved.

The silent, empty study felt intimate. I felt I was one clue, one hidden latch away from discovering the formula behind B.W.'s fortune. That capital spawns capital was no secret, but B.W. had always gone far beyond the usual dividends. He had maintained a statistically implausible hot streak for over two decades. I watched dark weather blow in from the north and did not hear Lens enter the room behind me.

Helen, he said.

Leo, I said. We briefly regarded each other. Specifically he regarded my slim gold dress, my big hair, my disco earrings.

You look . . . His hands indicated speechlessness.

Use your words.

Cleopatrian. Where's your Mark Antony?

Hew's on the other side, I said. I pointed down. From the window we could see the protest, about twenty minutes from getting soaked beneath incoming clouds.

The dusk cast an epic, menacing light. The sea looked like oil.

That's right, that's right, he's a man of *action,* said Lens.

He was nearly murdered at the last one. He had to take cover—came back with his hands all scraped up. You must have read what happened.

Lens held up his fine uncallused palms. And I, meanwhile... The hands do say a lot about a person. Is he all right?

Lens's concern was sincere, which was confusing. His expression was open, sympathetic, tender. I was not ready to meet it. I had been one-upping. I'd thought we were bantering. I'd thought we might veer our flirtation *away* from the subject of my maybe-spouse. I said Hew seemed fine, though we were currently at odds, as we some-times were in matters of political aesthetics. And you and I, I said, seem to encounter each other only at highly political times.

I've been in hibernation. Rarely seen and, when seen, not pleased about it.

A new book?

Always.

Coming along?

A protracted siege. Meanwhile Faulkner wrote *As I Lay Dying* in six weeks.

Perhaps you're no Faulkner.

Yes, the Nobel Committee keeps reminding me.

Regarding the Nobel, Lens was perennially overlooked. Some significant critics were on record saying he deserved it. My dad would have given it to him every year. Lens himself, I learned, did not think he *deserved* the prize so much as he resented the Nobel Committee's obvious political tint. For decades he had been out of bounds because the Committee found Jews, Americans, and sex— his three primary subjects—all rather too distasteful to celebrate regardless of the artistry with which they were portrayed. Later, his unjust Nobel ineligibility derived, my dad thought, from Lens being white, male, straight, old, and still American.

I said, You seem morose, old friend. Lens seemed substantially older than when I'd last seen him. He lacked the animation and ease I remembered—certainly he lacked the energetic command of his writing. Now it was his stillness that affected me, the calm way his bold brows and proud nose held the light of a nearby lamp. It felt as though Lens had authored the impending weather.

I'm in one of my blue periods. My whole life, he said, I have been making the exact same mistake. I keep coming to parties expecting to be enlivened, to have my mood shaken off me.

The experiment fails again, I take it? Definition of insanity and all that?

I've never understood that definition. My work is all try. Then try, try, try again.

Well, that's work. This is a party. We're celebrating.

Are *you* celebrating? he asked.

What do you mean?

I mean: Do you have a view on all of this? Lens captured the protesters vs. party in a glance. He said, You're both Cleopatrian and a sphinx to me. You think I haven't noticed you keeping your mouth shut? A noticeable political instability, an absence of outspoken commitments?

Let me get this straight, I said. You, Leo, want a person of my generation—apologies, my cohort—to be *more* explicit with my opinions? You want me to pick a side? And here I thought your problem with us was that we were too vocal, too black-and-white about everything.

You're unusual in many ways, Helen. Indulge me.

Wouldn't that ruin the suspense?

Some partygoers entered the study. They were not rowdy or drunk but still it felt like a violent interruption. I scowled at them. They wished to look at Yale of the past, would we mind?

Lens and I cleared out and were now by the exit, the antechamber. Lens seemed magnetically compelled toward the elevator, or else repelled by the ongoing social fray. He was not going back into the party. He said: I could use your help with something. A scientific consultation. I've been bothering Perry about it but maybe I'd rather bother you.

Another man, another invitation, another pretext. But this one I didn't mind. I said, Will I get into the acknowledgments?

No promises. It would ruin the suspense.

I'll have to be helpful, then.

Why don't you come visit me sometime?

I'd like that, I said. Where does one find you?

He described the house to me. I had walked by it ten times at least, unawares. He told me times of the week that would be convenient, that during these times there was no need to call ahead.

All right, he said, with finality, I'm turning into a pumpkin.

You used that line last time.

Damn, he said, another creative failure. Add it to my tab.

22.

Hew came home late. Soaked. The demonstration
had been over for hours. I was in bed, trying not to think
too much about Lens, and reading, or trying to read,
the latest addition to the latest fad in condensed-matter
physics. Every few years brought a new craze. Everyone
became convinced that some arcane subsubject portended
a breakthrough in high-temp superconducting. Physicists
are actually not much more rational than anyone else, so
this cycle had been repeating for decades. Perry and I
always worked our own angle. Still, I needed to keep up;
Perry relied on me for this; and tonight I was relying on
these papers as a sleep aid.

Hew grunted from the other room when I greeted him.
He came into the bedroom to change clothes, then went to
make himself tea. Then I heard his keyboard clattering.

What are you doing? I asked.

Work, he said. A lie, and meant to be understood as one.

Who've you been with?

Just protest people. You would have hated it, he said.

For a while I lay there—all the latest hottest physics flopped inert on our bedspread—imagining Hew touching the elbow of some virtuous Yalie. His long arms held a coat over her. They were running in from the rain. They were laughing about memes I hadn't seen, discussing news I hadn't followed.

When, in the morning, Hew made coffee without restarting our argument, I understood that I had done something really bad this time. Hew was as angry, as removed as he'd ever been with me. He was monosyllabic.

Later that afternoon, I thought he might have lightened a bit. He was splayed across the couch, his legs wide and askew, his arms and shoulders huddled close around his phone, and his face in a smarmy grin. This was his expression signifying that something really good was happening on the internet, and sometimes he liked to catch me up—though of course I never found anything as funny as I was supposed to. We called these Tales of High Culture.

I sat on the couch and said, What's the me-me?

He looked up at me and his face collapsed. His grin, his glee, teleported to Mars.

Oh, it's not content. I'm chatting.

Who with?

Not worth explaining, he said. They're just—you know, internet people, he lied.

So going to B.W.'s party apparently represented something dire—a betrayal. It could not, like coming to the Institute, be excused as part of my work, a necessary if distasteful measure in pursuit of a greater cause. It was not a symptom of my known obsessions or of other virtues. I had done something gratuitous. I'd exposed a dispute of values, grounds for civil war. With Lens I had called our differences a matter of political aesthetics, but of course this stuff was *not* aesthetics to Hew. That I thought of attending a celebration in B.W.'s penthouse as an aesthetic choice, while Hew heard it creaking with moral weight, was a core political division between us. It could not be papered over and probably could not be mitigated by compromise. Basically, I thought later, this was the moment I had clarified grounds for divorce.

And all this without Hew knowing that I intended to visit Leo Lens.

And all this before we found out that B.W.'s Thanksgiving party had coincided with, perhaps caused, one of RIP's more vivid and on-brand crimes. Hew and I argued about it for days—actually for months. The incident became a proxy war for everything else that was off-kilter between us, and the irony in all of this arguing was that Hew and I entirely *agreed* that she, the student—I'll call her Melissa—was telling the truth, and that he, the offender, the skeezy professor of English, was a rapist and a liar.

I had not noticed her at the party that night, but I had seen her around. She and I had noted each other several times in the dining hall—her quick blue eyes finding mine—and at least once had shared an elevator, which was how I knew she was tall.

The drama, Melissa's drama, played out as predictably as a procedural, with all the she-said-he-said tropes of a Supreme Court confirmation hearing. Melissa was compelling, detailed, restrained in manner. She kept her hair parted strictly down the center and clearly was not the sort of person who ever thought she would speak out on YouTube. She delivered a concrete and factual account, and for the most part held herself together until the end, when she said: I came here because I was not afraid. Everyone told me not to. But I am strong and I wanted to learn and be financially responsible and I just—I believe in people. I believe in second chances. And I'm saying that what happened to me—it, it wasn't right.

The professor's rebuttal, on the other hand, was vague, defensive, dismissive, outraged and—to Hew and me both—not credible.

So Hew and I agreed about the fact of the matter. We agreed that she was convincing and we agreed the professor should be prosecuted. But somehow we kept fighting about it. Apparently I agreed with insufficient passion.

Hew dug up some of this professor's old online posts— the reason he had been exiled to RIP—and threw them in my face. *I* had brought us to the Institute and then *I* had gone to B.W.'s party, so now apparently *I* had to defend this rapist's rather old-fashioned, rather French, vision of seduction. Basically the professor did not believe there was such a thing as coercion short of violence. In response to a friend's dismissal from another university, he had written a long thread along the lines of: power is erotic, what is verboten is erotic, never shall these elements separate until human nature alters, so we must learn to live with lop-sided power between sexual partners and with forbidden affairs gone sour. He offered some examples from classic literature. These were regressive and did not help the situation. The culminating, *coup de grâce* line was: "Yes, she thought her job might depend on it, that's why they *both* wanted to do it!"

These are your people, said Hew. These are the people you associate with.

No, these are the people *you want* to associate me with. I'm just trying to do my work the best way I can. The price, I guess, is some allies I don't want and some enemies I don't deserve.

I just don't see how you can be so . . . unmoved. How can you see something like this happening, you say you agree it's horrible—and then you do absolutely nothing different in your life? You won't march or demonstrate. You won't mention it to Perry or to anyone who matters.

What would that accomplish? Unless you can tell me what you expect reporting my feelings to Perry, or reporting them to the public on a piece of poster board, will accomplish, it would just be *vanity* for me. Or, worse, a kowtow to peer pressure. These issues fire your loins these days. Fine. But leave mine out of it.

So you'll just go on writing your code, living as if Melissa does not exist?

Individuality doesn't *mean* anything if we're obliged to spend our lives heroically lunging at every injustice. People do horrible things to one another all day, all the time, the world over. Why isn't it enough for me to do science? I'm trying to fix fucking *climate change*. Why do I have to be captive to every crisis? Why should I have to be in a constant state of broadcast, a pundit on every topic of public concern?

Is that what you think I'm doing all the time? I'm broadcasting?

What else would you call it? And that's what's maddening, Hew. We've established, I believe, that I agree with you. I would vote to convict. But *no one is asking* for my vote. What you really want is not my agreement but for me to be *vocal* about it, to buy into our cohort's infantile insistence on public display. As if every issue is so obvious and so simple and so salient that to do anything less than drop everything and scream your objection violates a moral imperative!

Yes, yes, I heard myself even in the moment: "cohort." The greatest hits of Leo Lens, spewing from my mouth. Hew was agog. And if Hew was agog just imagine my own surprise, my horror, at the thought that I might be becoming—dear god—a Conservative?

When had this happened? Was it possible that I actually believed what I was arguing? It certainly *felt* like I believed what I had said—but at the same time I felt sure I was missing something; surely I had somewhere overlooked a premise that would change my mind back? Political commitments of course are not like a coin collection: you can't open up a case and see them all laid out in some rational, coherent scheme and confirm—oh yes, I do have that one. Which coins do you have? But still it was alarming to feel that the ideas I heard myself advocating might lack any tether to broader convictions. But...what *were* my broader convictions? When Lens had asked for my political commitments, had I been playing at uncertainty — or was I actually not certain? Were my values really so malleable? Just a few months at RIP and, apparently, I was ideologically adapting without meaning to. I was assimilating.

Melissa went to the police, tolerated the rape kit and the whole humiliating inquisition. She explained how he had locked the door, how he had clutched her hair when she tried to pull away, how he had not seemed to hear her saying no, and how earlier in the evening, in B. W.'s penthouse, he had commented on her grades and a television internship to which he might connect her.

The professor of course claimed she'd wanted all of it, that she had been not just unafraid but eager, whatever her next-morning remorse.

The prosecutors pondered — was there sufficient evidence? Should this case be tried? The world awaited an announcement regarding the professor's indictment or lack thereof. Meanwhile the Institute issued the same statement it had used for prior, less vivid incidents: "The Rubin Institute Plymouth will cooperate with law enforcement, as always. The Institute does not otherwise intervene in or govern the social interactions of adults. All persons involved will be permitted to continue their studies and responsibilities at the Institute. Any dispute between or among such persons may be resolved privately or in courts of law."

All of it was so expected, so unsurprising. How could the needle of popular favor drift any further away from the Institute, you would wonder, given where it already was? But Melissa's video, her testimony, had been so vivid. So the Institute's indifference felt unusually blunt. You could hear the silence of former allies. You could feel public sentiment calcifying, losing nuance.

I mean, even I could feel it. I was becoming more attuned to this sort of thing, the way I always did when Hew and I were arguing. I went a bit more Online, dangled my feet in the current. I distracted myself with political fury like regular people did in regular jobs. It was one of several ways in which I was becoming unlike myself. Since when did I have the *capacity* to do the bare minimum at work, to leave HTS at the office? Since when had I excitedly attended parties, *dressed up* for parties? Since when did I take ponderous nature walks and read fiction? Since when did I extra-maybe-maritally flirt?

23.

The way stars form is slowly. They are an accumulation of mass and pressure. There is no match strike. First there are dust and gas, floating in space. If you were there it would feel empty. Some places there will be clumps of gas, a knot of atoms, dust bunnies. These have tiny gravity. Over a long time, gravity works. New dust and gas draw into the clump; clumps glom on to other clumps. The cloud gets larger. In the middle, pressure builds. *Eventually* the cloud collapses under its own gravitational attraction. Heat builds, atoms press closer and closer together, bouncing faster and faster. Eventually, not soon, there is a protostar. Eventually, not soon, the protostar becomes a star. For instance, our Sun, a perfectly average star, took about 50 million years to mature from initial gravitational collapse to the version we know. The sun is about 4.6 billion years into adulthood, which is expected to last another 6 or 7 billion years, at which point it will age into a calmer red color and, about a billion years later, burn out.

The universe itself is 13.77 billion years old, which means it took 9 billion years for enough dust and gas to gather to make the Sun.

Now these are no more or less than facts.

One thing that might occur to one, in light of these facts, is that change happens in rather small increments, or it doesn't so much happen as it *accumulates*. Dust approaches other dust—for 9 billion years. Eventually this dust is a star, powering life, something completely different. One cannot necessarily tell what change is occurring until well after it has occurred, and by then one is missing some new change.

Another thing that might occur to one is that *Homo sapiens* have existed only about 300,000 years, agriculture about 10,000 years, writing 5,000 years, the United States less than 250 years, *Brown v. Board* less than 80 years, the iPhone less than 20. One might think that the pace of human progress *feels* so *terribly* slow, but actually—

It might occur to one that "from dust to dust" is literally true—that we are star stuff. One might think that entropy governs all and that the fire of the whole universe will one day burn out. In the grand scheme of things, how could *culture* really matter? How could RIP matter, or one person like Melissa?

These are things that might occur to one who is pondering having an affair.

What one might want in such a circumstance is to think that anything one chooses to do, right or wrong, indeed one's whole life, is not even a blink in the life span of a dying universe. One might want to believe that one is always unalterably free, or unalterably not. One might want to believe that one's choices do not matter because they are not—or are merely—matter.

The point is that I did really think about it before I went to Lens's house. The moral valence did not escape me, as it apparently had regarding attending B.W.'s party. I minimized the moral charge by insisting that I had not yet decided to do anything objectively objection-able. I remained uncommitted regarding whether, if the opportunity arose, Leo Lens and I would be allowed to touch each other. All I had decided was to continue approaching circumstances in which that opportunity might or might not arise. The core issue was unripe for decision. Later, if necessary—and perhaps it would never be necessary!—I could decide what to do in the context of a live dispute, rather than in the ab-stract. This approach struck me as highly rational and judicious.

Still, on the walk to Lens's house I felt sick with myself, an apprehension near to the slow upward click of a roller coaster. Lens had issued an open invitation for after six on Wednesday, after six on Friday, or after five on Sunday. I had been perfectly available to go Wednesday or Friday but waited until Sunday. My delay was a power play, I suppose, but the discipline it required was psychologically important for me: I could not admit too much hunger, especially to myself. I had to establish control.

The island, now in winter, was brittle and dramatic. The leaves were off all but the scrub pines, laying bare the stark lines of hills, houses, and old rock walls against the sky. For once there was no wind. I heard my own heart and breath, my exertion up the light grade of Lens's slender road.

Hew thought I was at lab, if he was thinking of me at all. I thought about how Lens had said his erotic life was *kaput* and wondered whether this referenced an emotional state, presumably intractable, or a physiological condition treatable with tadalafil.

The house was neat, cozy, and plain, and would have seemed that way in 1979. There was a worn sofa, a long wall of books, yellow cotton window dressings, an oak table tattooed with moisture rings. The walls held hotel oil landscapes, as if Lens had once gone to a yard sale to find temporary, undistracting decorations—and these pictures had remained ever since. The living room window framed a modest view of a tan winter hillside, a stone wall, and the edge of the woods where I sometimes walked. Beneath the window stood a rolltop desk, the house's one extraordinary item. This was where Lens wrote. Its top was closed.

The house felt so familiar because I had read about it. Lens had described this place, some prior version of it, as the home of his late-life alter-ego narrator. So I knew it was an attempt, as he'd explained, at purity, serenity, simplicity, seclusion. An attempt to preserve all concentration and flamboyance and originality for the work, the calling.

I accepted an offer of tea and sat at one end of the worn couch. Lens placed a large glass teapot on a glass stand, above a candle. He took the room-dominant arm-chair. This had the view, the side table, the reading lamp. We were in position. Now, I thought, something should commence.

While I waited, a different thing was well underway. Lens sat there. He drank his tea. His gaze alternated between me and the view. For a while I catalogued his home goods, his books. I did not immediately realize that his silence was intentional, but as soon as I did realize it I became tense, uncomfortable. I could not decide whether Lens intended to provoke me to talk first, to establish that I was in the more deferential posture—which of course I was, having come to him during one of the windows he'd established—or whether he was genuinely at ease.

After quite some time, he said: You're a Jewess.

Half, but the wrong half.

I'm not doctrinal about these things.

Yes, I know.

Okay, you can't do that. Lens said this not sharply, not even firmly, but not kindly either. He said it instructionally, perhaps slightly frustrated that such a thing needed to be explained.

Can't do what?

You can't refer to whatever you know about me from my writing. It throws conversation off-balance. You may know things, and I may know you know things. But you must act as if you are discovering me as organically as I will be discovering you. Without that—Lens opened his hands—no waltz. Just a lot of toe-stomping.

Well, *that* is a disappointment, I said. I've been catching myself up on your *oeuvre*. I've been studying; it's what I'm best at. Now you tell me there's no test?

The test, if you must have one, is how well you can disassociate Leopold Lens from Leo. Those two are not the same and have never met, so it is pointless to talk to me about him.

What if I want to meet Leopold Lens?

He's a recluse. And a mute. He says what he means on the page. It takes time to get things down precisely, and once he manages to say something the right way he won't muddle it by speaking haphazardly on the same subject. Unless of course his editor requires him to do some publicity. But if you need Leopold Lens, you know the way to the library, *capiche*?

Lens sipped his tea, smirking slightly while I recalibrated.

I said: So you have science questions, you claim.

I do.

Are you writing sciency fiction?

More like an alternate history. One of my characters is a physicist, but I actually have no idea what he does for a living. I've used up my quota of scenes in which he pensively gazes through a telescope, meanwhile reflecting on cosmic meaning.

You're joking.

Not about writing a physicist. And if you don't help me I won't be joking about those grandiose reflections either.

"...That was when I realized, dear reader, that the true string theory, the string that mattered, was the one connecting the souls, hopes, and dreams of every person, the string that vibrates through all humanity..."

Forever and ever, amen.

I beg you, I said. Write that.

But actually string theory's a good place to start. Lens

leaned forward in his chair, his hawkish eyes crafting a sharp query. What—what is it?

Now it was my turn to say: You know your way to the library, right?

Humor me. I want to hear you explain so that I can see whether I've gotten it.

So for about twenty minutes we talked about string theory. It was impressive the extent to which he grasped the concepts and it was pretty clear, at the same time, that his math was not remotely strong enough to really understand it. He pressed me for analogies, metaphors, illustrations. But the primary difficulty with quantum phenomena is that they are completely unlike the phenomena of human experience and thus highly unfriendly to analogy. I found myself breaking down the Bekenstein-Hawking formula, and Lens's eyes displayed savage determination not to be bored—which of course meant he was, very.

I said, Isn't this, uh, pretty deep in the weeds for a work of fiction? Shouldn't you yada yada all this stuff?

I probably will, ultimately. But you can always tell when a writer suggests knowledge he doesn't in fact possess. It feels rickety, doesn't it? Too few bolts holding the thing down. This is a pet peeve of mine. You're grinning—a pet peeve of yours too, I guess?

The opposite. I *love* a montage. The spaceship is going to run out of oxygen, nothing to be done, but then a hardy scientist stays up all night—you see blueprints spread across the mess table, cups of coffee, his fingers run through his hair, oh the stress, and then *he's got it*! He's *invented* a way to manufacture oxygen using only common spaceship items! Connect the thingamajig to the whatchamacallit. Then you're on to the next plot point...What a fantasy. It's better than superheroes for me.

Interesting, he said.

But I will tell you a pet peeve. Though you'll think I'm an illiterate.

Out with it.

Why don't you writers write more about work? Not things that happen at work or things that happen because of work, but the actual *work*. The application of effort to a task; the thousands of little failures and successes and puzzles and tensions and et cetera et cetera. It's what most of us are doing most of the time. For many of us it is a sizable and significant piece of life. For a few of us it's the *most* important thing. But you writers can't seem to get interested.

Except in the work of writing. We love writing about writing.

Yes. So. Theorize this phenomenon.

We're pricks.

Come on, I said.

He shrugged. If we were interested in other jobs, we'd probably be doing those jobs. They'd certainly pay better.

Lens made us more tea. I went to the bathroom, checked my makeup, adjusted my blouse, sweater, and jeans. Lens had twice seen me dolled up, so today I'd decided to dress collegiate. It was impossible in this house, in his slightly musty green-tiled bathroom, not to feel that I was in a Lens story. I imagined myself in the role of Annette, Lisa, Sylvia—one of the sharp young women characters with whom the elder artist character inevitably has an affair; the ones he becomes enthralled with and subject to. This was the role I thought I wanted. But of course the one who really *understood* the elder artist was never the woman; it was always the *son,* the *protégé.* I wanted this too, and it would have been better casting, more appropriate on every level. All evening I hovered uncertainly between the two states, trying to blend them. Lens let me do this.

We talked for about two hours. Nearly everything he said about himself I already knew or had guessed, except for his current reading—a history of Morocco, in translation—and an enviably proprietary story about ice fishing with Bellow and Bellow's final wife. Generally Lens did not want to talk about himself; he wanted me to talk. I felt him mining me for information, chiseling for color in my life, and I did not mind. It had been some time since I'd last tried to summarize myself, to state my view of the world in general terms, as one must when dating. I never had much talent for this and I lost the skill completely once Hew and I coupled. But Lens asked the right kinds of questions. E.g.: Athens or Jerusalem? He cut to the heart of things. He grounded me. I felt much firmer in my identity than I'd lately been feeling with Hew. Lens was not visibly disturbed by my eventual admission—I was embarrassed not to be telling him but to only be telling him *now,* in the fifth or sixth hour of our acquaintance, the *delay* was what felt revealing—that my dad prayed daily at the Leopold Lens shrine. Hew was hardly mentioned. The Institute, Melissa's rape, mentioned only in passing.

In a lull in conversation Lens stood. Then I found myself departing.

Lens had not fed us, so I was famished. I salivated for illicit substances, for pulled pork, roast chicken, Vermont cheddar. In the brisk dark I descended the hill toward the Endowment. It glowed against the night and struck me for one absent, contextless moment as gorgeous. I was giddy, grinning behind my scarf, but why? I felt like I'd been kissed but nothing of the sort had occurred. We had done nothing. Our meeting felt distinctly unconsummated. I was not at all troubled by this.

Perhaps in fact this nonoccurrence was the cause of my giddiness? I was gaining a new intimate but at the same time we had preserved our potential. We had danced but learned nothing about our trajectory. I did not know whether I was part of a star forming or whether we were clouds of dust passing each other, mingling but never to be united. With Hew I had Schrödinger's wedlock; with Lens I now had Schrödinger's affair.

In the dining hall, I was almost alone. It was exam season. The few others present were sweatpants-clad, high-tension, coiled over laptops. I filled a tray with heaps of Brussels sprouts, mashed potatoes, a lentil and carrot stew. I shoveled it all down. I was a pillar of self-restraint.

24.

For weeks my work on the model had been, basically, adding complexity. Perry thought the last version had perpetuated rounding errors—when repeated millions of times, small inaccuracies add up—and that we had abstracted too much and in the wrong places. Hence me learning a new programming language to allow us to onerously calculate a value we had previously ballparked. Certain values needed to be changed from floating-point single-precision to double-precision format, which more than doubled accuracy for those variables but also doubled computing time. We unsimplified our parameters for disorder, superexchange, spin-orbit coupling, external magnetic fields, doping. All of this tended toward computational infeasibility, which it was my duty as numericist to prevent.

The simulation which had last taken 7.5 days would now, in its current form, require more than three weeks. This run time was about par for others in our line of work, but it was a lot longer than I was accustomed to. My code had always been high-performing, significantly more efficient than my peers'; some of my models could simulate 1000 atoms at the same speed that others simulated 200. Elegant and highly optimized code was the clearest way in which my talent manifested. It was irrefutable, and it was what had first brought me to Perry's attention. By contrast, the other form of talent in physics—extraordinary physical intuition, a la Einstein or Perry—typically can be identified only in retrospect, after an idea proves out.

Anyhow I was frustrated that our model was becoming so clunky, so conventional. Also so tedious to construct. I had said, Let me hone it down. I mean, disorder—we don't need that in double-precision. And all the other pieces I will have to build to get there? We're going to muddy the results.

No, no, Perry insisted. We can't simplify just for the sake of it. You have to allow for some mud. This obsession with efficiency can be counterproductive, Helen. We can't keep going through the motions of progress, running swift simulations that won't possibly work. No more shortcuts. We need to *learn* something.

I'd glared at him. Never mind, I guess, how much more work his way of doing things created for me.

Now it was almost the holidays. Perry called a meeting to discuss "our goals," as he put it, during vacation. I waited for him in lab for almost an hour before he finally emailed to say I should meet him at his bungalow.

I had not been to his house in perhaps a month. Meanwhile the parameters of Perry's life had apparently changed too. Evident on top of Perry's usual sloppiness was a marked increase in disorder, coupling, magnetism.

The living room bloomed with dishes and bottles, the odor of stale cheese and wine. Williams was in the kitchen, sautéing a breakfast of sausage, onions, and peppers. He greeted me apathetically, then brought two plates into the bedroom. Two plates? Through the wall I heard two voices—Williams and *another guy*. In Perry's bedroom.

Perry must have been indifferent to me seeing this, but I was too astonished to comment or to absorb anything else. I suppose I was a little possessive about Perry. Whatever he was telling me about this or that subroutine, the expected energy summaries, I heard it like the teacher's voice in *Peanuts*. All I could think about was how Perry—cerebral, condescending, unsensual, very rotund—now had two men in his bedroom and was acting as nonchalant as Keith Richards.

My immediate goal became to extend this meeting long enough to catch a glimpse of the other person in the bedroom with Williams. Was he an adult or another undergraduate? What sort of harem was Perry building here? I asked whether Perry was sure about how he wanted to represent insulation between cuprate layers. It was an important issue about which he was perpetually indecisive. He spent a while fussing with our code while I watched the bedroom door for signs of life.

Meanwhile there was this awful knotting in my chest.

Envy? Suddenly I felt carved out. I was aware of lack in my own life, the absence of certain intimate satisfactions that even *Perry* was now taking for granted. I don't think anyone loves to realize that others are having more sex than they are, but the real issue was not Perry having a couple of guys around. It was Perry's demeanor about the whole thing. Perry had always been, in my mind, an extraordinary but lonely man. His loneliness had provided some basis to believe that the fates do net things out; extreme ability on the intellectual axis came with weaker abilities on other axes. But here he was, so comfortably *complete*. He was inhabiting some kind of Aristotelian ideal of a well-lived life, and it seemed like he wanted me to see it.

And that knotting sensation: It was not quite envy but more like the feeling of driving a long stretch of dark highway and then realizing you've missed your turn. Oh—somewhere I must have missed a sign. Somewhere back there I must have had a chance to end up somewhere other than where I am, right? I *had tried,* hadn't I?, not to come to the Institute. In the end there hadn't *been* any other way—or was there? Because I now felt distinctly how many of my usual premises RIP had undermined: Hew and I were very on the rocks. HTS was these days more likely to put me to sleep than keep me up at night. I was so unsatisfied that I was plotting adultery with a man whose relevant organs were, in all likelihood, no longer up to the task.

Was I no more than a contrarian by disposition? In the normal world I had eschewed normalcy; I had no time for it. My life was HTS. This felt justified given the stakes. This felt justified given how little ordinary life had interested me. I'd thought this was my identity— an obsessive, a physics gunner defined by opposition to prosaic concerns. But now that I was in such distinctly unnormal circumstances, I'd been regressing to the mean. Like the new model Perry was making me build, I was revising myself into some clunky and bizarre version of conventional. Hew, ordinarily so well-adjusted, had grown increasingly deranged and antisocial; and I was deranging in the opposite direction, socializing with our despicable neighbors and arguing with utter conviction that Hew's committed virtue was childish and that I was *right* to be basically indifferent to the rape of a woman who lived not in some far-off country but in our same elevator bank, a woman who lived three floors below us and whose rapist lived twelve floors up.

Helen—are you all right?

Perry's wide eyes stared at me. He looked supremely uncomfortable.

Apparently I was sweating and for a while had been catatonic.

Through the bedroom door I heard chuckling and explosions and Samuel L. Jackson on television.

I muttered something about how Hew and I were fighting, that I was distracted, sorry. Maybe we can finish discussing later this week, after I get home?

Oh dear—okay—sure—of course, said Perry.

I hustled from the bungalow. A light snow had started falling. I did not take time even to zip my coat on the way out. I had to extract myself.

For most of five years, excepting the semester without Perry, I had been flourishing with unnatural purpose. The chores of graduate school had not been chores to me. I had been confident, because Perry was, that I would live up to my promise and ambitions. Perry had this sense of scientific destiny about him; it was unimaginable, once you knew him, that he would *not* invent something like ZEST. I attempted to project this same energy, and yes I knew I was talented in some ways...

But my ability to construct high-performing code felt, suddenly, rather pedestrian. It was not the same as physical insight, like Perry had. On Perry's mantel was a Nobel Prize and inside Perry's bedroom lay at least one, perhaps two, very attractive young men. They signified, were symptomatic of, I thought, the general magic that Perry had about him—and that I very much did not have myself. Why had I thought *his* destiny could rub off on *me*? I was in an intellectual class with fucking app developers, not with Feynman. I had turned down Google and J.P. Morgan, and then I had dragged Hew and myself into exile. I had compromised us—all on the assumption that I was or could become someone of Perry's caliber.

But now I knew what I had really done by coming to the Institute. I knew I would fail at everything: I would probably never regain my focus on HTS, and in any case I lacked the intellectual capacity to make it work; Hew and I would fall apart; my whole life would flounder. I would wind up alone, polishing algorithms in the bowels of J.P. Morgan. My newly reactionary politics would isolate me from educated society. I would probably get cats. All of this would be the cost of thinking I could *defeat* the Institute. This would be the price of my insistence that I was so strong, so independent, that I was so above culture and politics and human drama, above conventional wisdom, above the Online crowd, above Hew.

In the end I was just like everyone else at RIP: some-where along the line we'd all been sure that in my case, yes in *my* case, the rules would not apply.

25.

Accordingly I was glad for a change of scene. I needed distance, reflection. I could not yet tell whether my epiphany—this realization that the Institute had been a mistake, perhaps a bad one—whether this notion would last or dissipate. When you have radically changed and radically botched an HTS model as many ways as I have— with each failed change invariably based on a moment of seemingly blazing clarity—you learn after a while not to overcommit to each new insight. You do not immediately change the entire structure of your model. First you do a sanity check; you take a day or two. You throw together a quick estimation model on 40 or 100 atoms, a simulation you might run overnight on a regular PC, just to see if the physics play out remotely like you expect.

The holidays, I decided, would be my sanity check.

The ferry pulled away and I left RIP for the first time since August.

Hew and I never spent the holidays together. We would divide our forces this year too, per usual. He went to his family in Vermont, I to my dad in Maryland. In prior years, Hew and I had always reunited for New Year's Eve significantly more appreciative of each other, absence makes the heart grow and etc. — this was part of the point.

The other point was to prevent another explosion of the sort I had once caused in Hew's mother. The first time I visited Vermont I had spent the entire celebratory weekend, marking Hew's parents' thirtieth anniversary, on a code sprint, and I was allegedly rather rude to those who tried to interrupt or become even faintly acquainted with Hew's new girlfriend. All entirely in character for me, but a shock to Hew's family. Hew could have managed expectations better than he did. I now can't recall what I was working on that weekend. In any case, after 2.5 days of this, shortly before Sunday dinner, Hew's mother told Hew's father—her voice quavering, I overheard it, her first and perhaps to this day her only use of the word— that she thought I was a real cunt.

Later she and I made amends; now our relations were cordial. Still, it was best I did not visit during high-stress times. My otherwise lonely dad was my excuse to skip Hew's Christmas.

Hew watched the Endowment sink in the ferry's frigid wake. He cleaned his glasses twice and scowled into his phone. The atmosphere between us was Saturnian. He remained in his basic state of rage, and two days earlier I had witnessed something.

I had emerged from a basement stairwell into the Endowment atrium, intending a walk. And there was Hew—not hiding in our apartment, not working, but talking to someone. That center part, those swift, young eyes. Melissa. The back of Hew's neck in a tilt. An *interested* tilt? Was I witnessing their first encounter? Or had Hew's outrage on her behalf masked something—that he had a stake not only in justice but in *her*?

If I am not always socially attuned, I did in this instance immediately discern the cosmic logic—how elegant that would be, as inevitable as gravity. I had dragged Hew to this place where I pursued my own destiny with an iconoclastic Jewish novelist, and meanwhile Hew would meet her—*her*. A girl in need, with whom Hew would be as infinitely patient and tolerant as he was with me, but whose cause was far more sympathetic. I was beyond repair; here was a girl he could try to fix. A girl with whom he already shared a common enemy, who proved a point, and whom one simply could not hate, though for the moment I was managing it. Melissa's blue eyes, the genteel strength of her bone structure, her height—she already looked like a member of Hew's family. A fit.

I had watched them for thirty seconds, maybe, before I could no longer stand it.

Of course this was not something I could mention under present conditions, though it was hard to think of much else. On the ferry, I studied Hew's long face as he gazed down into his hand, scrolling.

At the New Haven pier, demonstrators were out in force. With Melissa's rape still front-of-mind, many signs had abandoned cleverness and said only some variation of Shame.

The car-rental shuttle-van pickup zone was right in front of the protesters. While we waited, Hew turned and thanked them, shaking some hands in solidarity, waving to one person he'd apparently met at Thanksgiving. It was *so* important that they were all *still engaged,* out even in *cold weather, keep fighting.* I wanted to punch him, and I kept wanting to punch him all the way to Hertz and for a couple of hours after we parted ways, heading in opposite directions on I-95 in matching Ford Fiestas.

26.

The old house — every visit I had to brace myself. My dad was neither miserly nor an ascetic, but the house said otherwise. Dad had an allergy to home maintenance. He refused to enter a Home Depot—part of a principled yet visceral rebellion against the football-commercial idea that men, in the absence of crops and animals, should instead continually grout, paint, acquire and organize power tools, retile bathrooms, and construct decks with custom fixtures for huge grills and Jacuzzis. The premise of these advertisements struck him as exactly as ludicrous as women supposedly *requiring* diamond jewelry, which he similarly opposed on principle.

So while Dad spent generously on food and wine and books and concert tickets, conditions at home idled at the point of minimum functionality. What qualified as minimum functionality was of course a matter of my dad's tolerance for inconvenience and discomfort, which had grown over the years, with the house deteriorating accordingly. The driveway was now unusable. It could have been resurfaced for perhaps $2,500, but instead for ten years Dad had been parking on the street. The house was about 160 years old, and the radiators in the two up-stairs bedrooms had never worked in the time we owned it. These might have been replaced for perhaps $1,500. Instead we used space heaters and depended on warmth from downstairs drifting up through fissures in the wide-plank floors.

Dad shoved through the kitchen door, took my duffel, and brought it upstairs. Since I'd last been here, several cabinet doors had detached and now stood propped, hinges dangling, on the floor beneath the shelves they were supposed to conceal.

My first hours at home were always a war with myself. On the one hand I wanted to nag Dad about all the annoyances and disrepair, all the stuff Hew would have long ago fixed. One of the privileges of my gender, I sup-pose, was that I had no beef with Home Depot. Pressing Dad toward home improvement felt for some reason like a daughter's duty, like I was establishing that I cared about the condition in which he lived.

On the other hand I didn't, really. He was a grown man, cognitively able (if not, in my opinion, entirely sane), and if he was satisfied with his own house I had no warrant to interfere. If I started nagging and tidying we would just have to play out a clichéd dynamic, me performing invasive caring, him performing resistance to same. We had done this a few times over the years; it was tiresome and pointless.

Dad came back downstairs and said, I have to get Patricia at the MARC train.

Okay, I said.

Need anything at the pharmacy? Any groceries?

No.

Okay, he said. There's coffee in that cabinet. He pointed toward the cabinet where we had kept the coffee for twenty-five years.

While he was gone, I satisfied my itch to improve things by washing a few windows and tightening bolts on the kitchen stools. I felt better and probably he would not notice any change. After this I skimmed through the model. It continued to bore me intensely—there were about a thousand things to check and tweak, and this was too many, so I did none of them. For an hour I pretended to study Fortran, which I now knew almost well enough to write the bottleneck subroutine. Of course I was not really thinking about any of these things as I did them. I was thinking Melissa, Melissa—what was the nature of their relationship? How had they met? Was he texting *her* right now?

Patricia arrived. We hugged, withdrew, and then she and Dad stood in the hallway grinning at me. Her blond hair was bound in a beige fleece headband, and beneath her coat she wore the green merino sweater I'd given her for Christmas last year. She was terrifically thoughtful and gracious—a necessity for anyone dating Dad—and she was waiting for me to notice the compliment she had paid me.

I said, Oh, nice sweater!

Well, since two of us are bundled up already, how about a walk? Patricia said.

A great idea, a relief. If we were at home, otherwise idle, supposedly we should be conversing. But on a walk we would already be doing something. Perhaps fresh air would extract me from my daze. Dad and I always learned the most about each other in the middle of other things.

It was the eve before Christmas Eve. The air was temperate, midforties, a little humid. The neighborhood was as jolly as it could be. Our locale was neither Baltimore nor DC—it was uncut Maryland exurb. It was not very rich or very poor. It was diverse but not to a point worth advertising. Our town remained surprisingly robustly Catholic. But this was not something one could discern at a glance. One town over, meanwhile, was essentially a joint suburb of Beijing and Mumbai, filled with NSA cryptographers and their families. The most obvious feature of our neighborhood, like Dad himself, was a kind of dignified disrepair. Most houses were very old and had been rebuilt piece by piece, like Ships of Theseus with new garages. Still, everything tilted and creaked; replacing parts could not erase plantation history or the way a structure had settled into the land.

I've been rereading *The Grouse,* Dad said. This was one of the more recent Lens novels. It's just remarkable, the compression but also—

The accumulation, I said. All that description of architecture, but such longing behind it, the way he makes objects, like—

He makes objects transmit ideas, Dad said. *Yes.* And the scene with Nadya in the stairwell . . .

I know, I said.

And here I thought you were all work, no time for reading, out there on your island.

I had not told Dad about meeting Lens and sensed it would be too abrupt to tell him now. The disclosure waited like an unexcavated bomb.

Pat won't read Lens anymore, he said. She says he's too angry at women.

We walked in silence for a minute.

Oh, how's Hew?

Fine, I said.

Patricia said, So tell me about your project, Helen. You've moved to—to that place. But you are still working on the same wires thing as before?

I said that yes, it was the same wires thing.

And I know you've told me, but what exactly is the problem with the wires we have?

I explained about electrical resistance, how even in the most conductive materials there is friction between electrical current and the substance through which it wants to flow, how basically electrons are always getting caught or hitting things or bouncing off in the wrong direction, which means a lot of energy is not getting from point A to point B.

Okay, she said, and now tell me what you do every day over at—at that place. You're trying to make better wires?

Indirectly, I said. We are trying to figure out the

underlying physical principles that will tell us how to make materials that might eventually be used to make better wires.

Okay, she said. And how do you figure out a physical principle?

I tried, and I really did like her, but we had never found a conversational level on which one of us did not wind up alienated. She was always *so interested* in my work. But the more I tried to explain about the Hubbard model, Cooper pairing, density matrix renormalization group algorithms, and how these were less precise than exact diagonalization algorithms but were the better tool for capturing interesting physics in 200+ atoms given existing computational bandwidth, the clearer it became to both of us that we lived on different planets. She nodded diligently, her face eager and begging for mercy.

Then I asked about her work at the Baltimore National Aquarium, where she volunteered. Per usual she started into an anecdote, some crisis with the sharks, and then cut herself off, apologizing for boring me.

The more I insisted that I did want to hear about it, the more she deflected and said I was very sweet to ask. I was impotent to communicate that I was not and never have been sweet, but I *was* in fact interested in sea creatures, and in the National Aquarium in particular.

27.

The aquarium, more than any other setting, felt like my mom. Dad must have had this association too and it must have had something to do with him and Patricia.

Mom had taken me there a lot when I was little. In retrospect it was quite extravagant, how often we went, given what I now recognized to be its exorbitant price. This was back when Dad still worked at a larger firm, which meant both that he was often absent on weekends and that $136 per week in aquarium fare was fiscally plausible.

I was a glutton; I would have gone every day. I dreamed of getting trapped inside, of living in there. It turns out there are many precocious girls who decide at some point that they will be marine biologists, an aspiration so common it's a cliché and—guilty. Though I think I committed to this career, and abandoned it, earlier than most.

I have never had one of those moments where my mom's face comes to me in memory, speaking tender wisdom.

A lot of what I remember is not quite memory; it is inference from stories, photos, and footage. Other than this I remember strange things, the wrong things. I remember dragging her up Pier 3 toward the aquarium, the way its sharply geometric structures loomed like a great prow in Baltimore harbor. I remember how she used to hand me a pencil and the black-and-white marbled comp notebooks in which I recorded my personal classification of marine species. Then Mom would put on headphones, connected to a Discman in her purse, on which she listened to audiobooks while I went from tank to tank, noting key observations that would eventually add up, I was sure, to a phylogenetic breakthrough.

Even if I learned something very interesting, I was not to interrupt Mom's "reading" but was instead supposed to wait and report all my new findings in an efficient, organized form, on the drive home. In retrospect: a prelude to presenting scientific papers, and perhaps one reason I was such a natural. At the beginning my core interests were mainstream—the Atlantic bottlenose dolphin, the leatherback sea turtle, puffins. Later I trended toward the obscure, toward corals and deep-sea crustaceans.

Like I said, I remember the wrong things. Teachers tell you what you are supposed to retain; it is *new* knowledge, new skills, not daily experience, that you make an effort to file away. No one tells you to memorize, in case of pulmonary embolism, every passing phrase of the most obvious and consistent element of your life. So I remember hardly anything Mom ever said to me. But

I do recall that the Valvatida order of starfish contains 16 families, 172 genera, and 695 species; that octopus tentacles have chemoreceptors allowing them to taste by touch; that the tasseled wobbegong, *Eucrossorhinus dasypogon,* is the only known member of its genus.

Anyway.

28.

On Boxing Day, I realized that Hew and I had entirely forgotten to text or talk on Christmas Day. Or perhaps it had not been a matter of forgetting.

Two days later, the public learned that the Knights of Right, the assaulters of Philadelphia, were apparently great fans of RIP and B.W. Rubin. Some documents had leaked out of the prosecutors' investigative file. CNN accessed the logs of a private rightist forum, where the topic of debate was whether B.W. could be considered an ally of the Knights.

On the Pro side: B.W. was against PC bullshit like the Knights were, and his Institute was Western education done right. The Knights wanted to send all their sons *and* daughters to RIP.

On the Anti side: B.W. was a kike.

Dad's take was that everyone on earth would benefit if we all cared less about what occurs on college campuses.

But, well, some of us have to spend our entire lives on

college campuses, I said. It was morning and I sat cross-legged in the dim corner of the couch with my first cup of coffee. Dad floated in his enormous electric recliner—a gaudy, stained, leather monstrosity. Beside his chair were tables and lamps, one of each on each side. He claimed the two lamps balanced his light for reading. The two side tables were overloaded with books and newspapers, open to crosswords that Dad had started but not yet completed.

It's okay for kids to be crazy at college, he said. That's what college is for. The problem is that now no one is forcing them to grow up after college. They become employees; they move to New York and work in media. They work on political campaigns. But no one tells them to shut their traps. So we end up with an entire country that has the culture of a college campus, when actually it's all child's play. No serious person could take it seriously.

So, I said, you think the Institute is a good thing?

If it's letting you do your work, it must be a good thing. How many times have I said: Great men, great people, are rarely good. Do we want, say...Do we want Keith Jarrett to stop playing piano just because he's a prick? Of course not. We should be *squeezing* the talent out of these people. Who cares whether they're happy, successful—what should we care? It's not about what they have for themselves; it's about what they, what *you,* can give to the rest of us. Why should we impoverish *ourselves*?

So what's good for the goose is good for the gander, and these special people are the geese and the rest of us are the ganders. Is that right?

All I'm saying, Dad said, is that we want fertile conditions for creation. We don't want to get in our own way. That's all.

Hew and I are in a real spat about this, actually.

Dad looked surprised, and I was surprised at myself. It was not like me to let Dad in on the Helen-Hew dynamic. It was not the kind of thing I discussed, full stop.

Is . . . everything all right?

If he had not asked so directly, so broadly, I might have told him what was going on. I might have said: Can we take a walk? And then we might really have talked. Dad could be good in a crisis. When in high school I had, after months of passive-aggressive bullshit, finally fallen out with Jenny Levine, Dad had taken me for a drive around Ellicott City and by the end I'd made my peace with the whole thing.

But now I looked at Dad, the slightly fearful concern on his face, and I just couldn't. I couldn't discuss Hew, couldn't say what I feared RIP and Melissa ultimately might represent in my life. The whole thing was too fraught, too consequential to stare at directly. And uncorking any one issue might mean a natural flow into everything else that was happening with Perry, with my tattering focus, and of course with Lens—a secret that would send Dad into conniptions. Some part of me feared Dad might *want* me to lose Hew, whom he had never particularly adored. Some part of me wondered: Would he want me to sleep with Lens? Wouldn't entering the Lens universe, becoming a Lens character, seem to Dad like a high achievement?

I said, We're in a rough patch, but it will be fine. It happens.

Later that morning, I finally called Hew. Mostly I just wanted to hear his voice. When he picked up he was panting. Out running. I could picture him, bound in fleece and spandex, pounding along pastoral Vermont roads, his breath coming through his balaclava like exhaust, his eyes meeting the gazes of indifferent goats.

How far are you going?

Seven, maybe nine, he said. This was telling. Anything over five miles for Hew was a psychological endeavor, not about fitness.

You can call me back.

If I wanted to call you back I wouldn't have picked up.

It's nothing urgent. Just wanted to talk. You probably saw the news.

Are you all right? he asked.

Am *I* all right?

Can't have been easy to read all that. I'm sorry. I should have called. I didn't know if you were up yet.

Why wouldn't I be all right?

You know . . . "kike." All those swastikas.

My heart gaped for Hew, and broke too. The Knights had pretty nearly murdered Hew, personally, and here he was concerned that their swastika gifs would perturb his Semitic partner. It was such a stupidly *correct* notion to think of one's Jewish loved ones at such a time, straight out of the progressive empathy handbook. At the same time, it was so incredibly incorrect as it pertained to me specifically. How could Hew have thought *I* would not be all right? You would think that only if you hardly knew me. Had all my Helen-ness, my particularity—everything Hew ought to have known of my personality, my beliefs, my resilience—been washed out, in his mind, by the bare fact of Jewishness?

The Knights of Right don't love Jews. Shocker. Are you upset?

I'm fine, he said. I mean these fuckers are just—

Are you furious?

I could hear him shrug. He said, I dunno . . . I'm so angry already, I don't know how much worse it could get.

I said, I miss you.

Yeah, you too, he said. I'm gonna keep running.

The state of our union must have been pretty bad, given that I left this conversation feeling better.

29.

Now if only B.W. had kept his mouth shut. No one expected him to go out of his way to publicly denounce or disavow the Knights. All I'd expected, all I'd hoped for, was that he would decline to comment.

What B.W. did instead was offer admission to two young men who had been outspoken on the Knights' forum and, upon its publication, were expelled from their colleges in a matter of days. Both guys had applied to the Institute in high school but lacked the academic qualifications. However, good grades apparently were no longer required if one was sufficiently ideological, which in this case is to say sufficiently racist, misogynist, and anti-Semitic. One of them had written fan fiction about what if "we" hadn't lost the Civil War.

B.W. did not merely offer them admission; he did it in the *Wall Street Journal*. His op-ed: "Two Young Men Called Me a 'Kike.' Now I'm Paying for Them to Attend My University."

The substance was a holier-than-thou stick in the eye about the transformative power of education, how people cannot ever truly be expelled from society, how our institutions must learn to accommodate reprehensible viewpoints, how the people we find most repugnant are those it is most important to understand and work to change. Thus he was going to give these young men, who had been abandoned by other supposedly liberal educational institutions, a place to learn and grow. All of this was generic, forgettable First Amendment stuff. What turned out to be memorable, in retrospect, was B.W.'s extended metaphor about the Endowment:

When I founded the Institute, we needed more space. We could have built numerous small structures— separate dorms, labs, and academic departments— spread out around the campus. But I did not want people to live in silos. I wanted people and ideas to intermingle, to be on top of one another. So we built up instead of out, one building instead of many.

This was no easy task. We were on an island made of brittle rock. There would be gale-force winds and violent storms. So the building could not be brittle. It had to be resilient against these unrelenting natural forces. To make it work, we had to dig deep into the rock—to root ourselves—and then to engineer a cutting-edge, flexible internal core—a spine that would bend but never break.

When people look at the building, now known affectionally as the Endowment, I hope that is what they see: a place built with tremendous effort and human ingenuity, and a place—a society—that is strong enough, and forgiving enough, to accommodate the high winds of human illiberalism...

Dad read the op-ed aloud to me while I was packing up. He was really moved by it; he was sold. He said, incredulous, Hew really doesn't see the virtue in this?

30.

I drove north, dropped the Fiesta in New Haven, boarded the ferry almost alone. A bleak and wet day. The ferry's heat on overdrive. I sat in the cabin, sweating, unable to see through the steam- and rain-drenched windows. Progress toward home—did I really think of RIP as *home*?—was marked only by jostling and swaying, changes in engine pitch. At the wharf, in the 4 p.m. dark, I hailed an autonomous cart and rode up toward B.W.'s huge boner for liberal values.

The Endowment lobby was empty. I had returned pre-semester; undergrads remained away. I had never seen the atrium truly vacant. I had never before felt I could sit there undisturbed and enjoy the vast dim architecture. I dwelled a moment. The machine made me a coffee. I slumped into an armchair by the window and watched the rainy lawn, trees keening in gusts. An exhausted peace settled around me, almost postcoital. The Endowment, the whole island, felt like the site of high drama and rich memory—but all of it made distant, all of it completed, or so I hoped, by the passing of one semester into another.

The elevator dinged and a moment later B.W. was with me in the atrium. He did something on his phone, hailing a cart, I assumed.

Then he was approaching. Something felt distinctly nonaccidental, as if he had intended to find me here.

B.W. took the chair opposite mine. The Endowment atrium was glass, steel, and concrete, but I suddenly felt surrounded by mahogany paneling. It remained impossible to really discern B.W., though I could notice details: the perfect crispness of his trousers, his monogrammed cuffs, the prim way he crossed his legs, the grotesque whiteness of his teeth. But the whole picture was like looking through the ferry window had been—a fogged suggestion of something vast.

Helen, he said. You're back early.

He maintained firm eye contact. It was disturbing. Besides a shrug to acknowledge that yes, the semester had not started yet, there were so many things to say to B.W. today that it was not possible to say anything at all.

How much longer before you run another simulation?

A few weeks, I said, which was how long I'd promised Perry it would take me to clean up the new version. It was possible to imagine unintrusive ways that B.W. would know so precisely what Perry and I were up to—we'd had to publicly schedule our time on the supercomputer,

160

and perhaps he'd seen that; or perhaps Perry and B.W. had bumped into each other over the holidays?—but B.W.'s demeanor undermined benign explanations. His knowingness was not casual. He meant me to understand that he had sources, that I was in his domain, that I was surveilled.

I thought he should know I was aware of at least some of *his* movements. I said, I saw your piece in the *Journal* this morning.

You keep up with the *Journal,* do you?

I keep up with what pertains to me. Well, that's not quite true, but in this case...

What do you think?

What about?

Should I have admitted those young men or not?

Yeah, I said, I think we'll all learn a lot from them.

I had not set out to be rude but rudeness was coming naturally. I channeled Hew. I was already imagining telling Hew about this and wanted to be the protagonist when I did.

If B.W. had a sense of humor about himself, it was not in evidence. At the same time, if I had provoked him, this was not in evidence either. He deployed the same extractive gaze he had used when he visited the lab, like he was appraising me for resale.

He said, So the piece did not persuade you?

Oh, you can't really have expected to persuade anyone.

What if I told you I was a simpleton about these things? That I am an idealist and believe absolutely in the power of rational thought and common human interest.

I don't think I'd believe you.

Why not? B.W.'s fingers drummed his armrest.

Because you could have admitted the two Nazis without announcing it in the newspaper. Because you arranged for your Thanksgiving party and a huge protest to occur on the same day. These strike me as decisions intended to produce a limbic reaction.

A *limbic* reaction, he repeated. Now B.W. grinned. His smile was not an improvement. I felt as if I had either passed or failed an exam but would never find out which.

An autonomous cart pulled up outside the window, and B.W. stood and adjusted his coat.

You are going to change the world, he said, far more than I ever will. A few more weeks...

B.W., I said, why—why do you care about this? About HTS, I mean.

He looked surprised, almost hurt.

This is the one planet we've got, he said. We're all in this together, aren't we?

I went upstairs and stripped naked without further ado. I was in pressing need of a shower. The day's travel and this second strange encounter with B.W.—this interrogation—had coated me in some hideous residue. I stood in the shower a long time, de-griming myself with pumice and microbead soap, like I had swum through an oil spill.

While I air-dried, I pulled out my laptop and scrolled through code. For a week with Dad I'd procrastinated, promising myself I would reengage with work when I returned to the Institute. It was time to make good. But

I'd lost the thread. The model felt foreign, like someone else's. The work I still had to do was very bland: revising subroutines per Perry's vision and then, through the whole model, tediously tracking every variable for purposes of memory management and ensuring appropriate double vs. single precision. Often the fun in my work was in finding clever little optimizations along the way, but I was blank, an empty tank.

Instead I slipped into bed and masturbated. I would like to be sufficiently evolved that I have no shame about this, but I'm not and I do. I require absolute privacy. Hew cannot be on the premises. There must be essentially zero possibility of interruption, even by a phone call. I can't shake the feeling that whoever calls can somehow sense what I'm up to. It was categorically impossible to do it in Maryland, where you could hear a sigh throughout the whole house and Dad's schedule was opaque: he was always getting home much earlier or much later than I expected. I had to seize these opportunities where they arose, and the seams at the edge of travel were good moments. Presently Hew was not even to New Haven yet; Perry did not know I was back on campus; I'd already informed Dad of my safe-and-sound arrival.

So I was sufficiently alone. I felt activated, lecherous. I took my time; I luxuriated in it. The pleasure I gave myself was significantly above average. I am sure, in retrospect, that this had something to do with the fear B.W. stoked in me. I'd sensed his general worldly power, of course, but I must have also sensed his sexual menace. It was not until after I was done, when I had dressed and remade the bed and reopened my laptop, that it occurred to me just how invasive B.W.'s surveillance might be. For a few minutes I scoured the apartment for pinhole cameras, finding nothing in the vents but dust bunnies.

31.

In the morning I woke to rustling: Hew, who had gotten in late and gotten up early, trying to be quiet. Trying to let me sleep. I heard him leave the bedroom on the balls of his feet, gently pulling the door closed, slowly releasing the knob to avoid a click. He was so considerate; a reflex for him. In return I'd done the considerate thing, letting him think he hadn't woken me. For a few minutes I lay there wafting warm thoughts in his direction. I wanted him to return with two cups of coffee and climb back into bed. It was a new year. Through the door I called, Darling?

I said it again, louder.

Hew had gone out.

When he returned he did not volunteer where he had been all morning—or with whom. I did not ask because he might tell me.

Instead I told him about the bold, contrary things I had said right to B.W.'s face. Apparently, however, I still showed inadequate conviction. I tried to describe the encounter with undertones of disgust and peril, but it came out forced, melodramatic.

Sure, Hew said, barely looking up from his phone. The whole thing sounds weird. But I don't see what you're trying to prove. We don't agree about this place. So it goes.

What do we disagree about? What do I have wrong? I said. Now I was determined to pick a fight.

He exhaled with great forbearance. The same thing that's always wrong, he said. You won't act. You're not, actually, convinced. You won't commit yourself to anything unless it's been proved up by the scientific method, unless it's a collection of well-tested, falsifiable propositions. But I don't know how many times I can tell you that not everything is like that. Values are not like that. You keep waiting for the debate to end in consensus. But this dust never settles. Sometimes you have to decide what you believe with insufficient evidence. Sometimes you must act on imperfect information. All I want is for you to *do* something about what you claim you believe.

Otherwise, he said, you're just a champion of the status quo.

And therefore a hypocrite.

Your words, Hew said.

Spending all day on your phone is what you consider to be *action*? You know that I can't stand looking at all your feeds, all your posts and takes? I just can't do it. The way you are out there just trying to *keep up*. It's . . . mortifying. It's like when a popular girl wears Ugg boots to school for

the first time, and the next week there's you and everyone else with Uggs of your own. I mean...Ugh. Maybe
politics isn't science and never will be, but it shouldn't be
entirely a matter of fashion either.

For a couple of days after this we didn't really talk.
He furled himself into his phone with daunting intensity,
and I went to lab a lot. There was much to do on the
model but I was further from focus than maybe I had ever
been. On a little laptop screen I watched whatever the
algorithms nudged me to watch, mostly big stupid movies
with big stupid heroes and big stupid aliens, and all that
seemed to separate the heroes from the aliens—in moral
terms, anyway—was that the aliens cared only about ends,
some grand ultimate vision, while the heroes sometimes
cared about means.

One morning I offered an olive branch. I put my hand
on the back of Hew's neck and ruffled his light curly hair.
I said, Should we talk?

What good would that do?

We might work through it. What's the good in *not*
talking?

The good in not talking, he said, is it allows me to
tolerate being in the same room with you for more than
an hour at a time.

Jesus, Hew.

I'm sorry, he said. That's where I am.

I'm not sure I would call your demeanor tolerant. It's
like you're shut up in a little box.

Are you serious? he said. This is why I haven't wanted
to talk.

What did I say?

Are you really saying *I* have to be more present? Consider that what you're feeling now is how I feel *all the time*. You spend your entire goddamned life in a box. Either you're in your head about HTS or you're yukking it up with Perry; regardless it doesn't include me. Just—just let me be, for a while, would you? I think I'm entitled to some privacy in my own head.

A few days after this I noticed that Hew wanted privacy somewhere else too. I went to change the music he'd put on and he had changed the passcode on his phone. Normally we were open-device.

Not long after this I noticed him wearing headphones around the house. Hiding in plain sight.

And soon thereafter I felt something invisible but glaring. He seemed relaxed. I watched his big veiny feet, on the coffee table, metronoming whatever music he had on, and it was not lost on me that I was watching Hew enjoy a song more than he had enjoyed me in months. Of course I did not really think it was the song causing his light mood, but it was impossible to raise the real issue neutrally— without starting something or, perhaps, ending it. Melissa. Whoever he kept messaging. I was paralyzed. Soon I could not even *get* him to fight with me about politics anymore. I sensed secrets obstructing us, and I thought I knew their names, but he now seemed determined to be passive, never to engage.

At first I was puzzled and then after a few more days I thought, Oh. Hew is going to leave me.

It was like learning a correct theorem. The hypothesis

that Hew planned to leave gave sense, an organizing principle, to otherwise strange and complex phenomena. He was becoming jarringly *collegial*. He left snacks out for me at night; he was scrupulous about the dishes. Hew was acting, I realized, like an expatriate in a country he would soon depart: its problems would not materially affect him in the long term—our life would not be *his* life—and accordingly provided little motivation to fret. He was divesting and had decided, how Hewish, to be professional about it.

32.

One of my tendencies, when I am in turmoil, is to become hyperrational. I mean even more than normal. What I do is I pretend, for my own benefit, that I am and can be analytical on a Spockish level. Hew once described this behavior as "truly chilling." Its psychological roots are not mysterious. Mom died and the only thing that really took my mind off it was math, coding. I discovered hyperfocus. I abruptly abandoned marine biology. The various species of jellyfish I had been studying were intolerably close to *Homo sapiens,* a species I at that point wanted nothing to do with. Everything in the aquarium or mentally adjacent to it was drenched in Mom's presence, submerged in her. Dad let me put something in the casket to be cremated with Mom. The chosen objects: my aquarium comp notebooks.

Then of course it turned out I had more than an aptitude for math, once I was applying myself. A star was born. Shortly I started skipping grades.

So, anyway, this was my mode when facing a loss—this time, loss of Hew. I sequenced my thinking.

The first question, which would define the rest of the strategy, was whether I perhaps *preferred* him to leave. I could not rule this out without thinking it through. After all, hadn't I been, wasn't I still, flirting with an affair? Hadn't *I* been uncertain about what I wanted? No one likes to be dumped. So if we could reach basic agreement that our maybe-wedlock had run its course, there was no reason to cling to it. Obviously mutuality was preferable if it was possible, as it would simplify all subsequent questions that arise from a split, or would at least reduce their stakes.

This determination of what I wanted, like apparently all of my models these days, became inelegant and unwieldy. Whether to stay in a partnership is quite a complex question, if you assess it truly *de novo*. I thought this was probably one reason people made the formal commitments that Hew and I had so far only toyed with. The existence of a commitment would have simplified the problem I was now addressing. A commitment would have swamped other factors, because fidelity to such commitments carried such well-understood moral weight and social benefits, whereas lack of fidelity to same . . .

But now suppose there is a conspicuous lack of said commitment. Now suppose that the other partner will not necessarily be hurt by the choice to wind down the association, indeed that he might be pleased or relieved. In other words: Remove the commitment factor and the question gets much closer, much harder to predict. It is not the kind of simulation you can throw together overnight.

Pro/Con lists are bush-league. What I did was generate a list of potential outcomes from breaking up, each of which had a positive or negative cardinal value, e.g., +1 or -2. Each outcome also had a likelihood between 0 and 1, representing the percentage chance that this particular outcome would in fact occur. Once I had the base value and likelihood of each outcome, I multiplied base by likelihood, then summed the total. For a while I could do the math in my head almost as fast as I could fill in an Excel. A result above 0 meant split, below 0 meant stay.

So at first the calculation was a breeze. What took some time, some thought, was cataloguing likely effects and assigning base values and likelihoods to each.

For instance, there were some effects, like living alone, where it was not even clear whether the value should be positive or negative, never mind *how* positive or how negative. In such cases I had to break the effect down into components that could each be valued more confidently. So instead of considering living alone as a single factor, I considered its components: having no one to talk to at home (-6), not having to talk to anyone at home (+3), sleeping alone (-3), being messier than Hew prefers (+1), no one cooks (-1), unapologetically controlling my own schedule (+4), no more Hew smell (-2, I loved his smell), and so on. These factors just mentioned were, in fact, on the simpler side, because they were certain to occur and all thus had a likelihood of 1.

More complicated were secondary and tertiary effects, such as whether having no one to talk to at home and controlling my own schedule would lead to a state of untenable social isolation, and if so how long this untenable social isolation might last, and similarly whether untenable social isolation might lead to productive improvements in my work and commitment to same, which if they made a marginal difference in scientific progress toward widely available planet-saving HTS-based technology would plainly be worth almost any cost to me personally. Once I had everything in Excel it took three minutes to write the script that would do the calculation automatically and show the result in a cell at the top, allowing me to fiddle as much as I pleased and see how new factors drove the total.

Other factors to consider included, for instance, whether I would find anyone who suited me better than Hew, whether this person might be Leopold Lens, whether splitting with Hew might facilitate more earnest and open exploration of potential with Leopold Lens, and whether—if the new person was *not* Leopold Lens—he could be found at RIP or whether I would have to go elsewhere. Or whether I might be alone in perpetuity, given the known difficulties I present to any relationship, and whether this was positive or negative, given same.

Another factor to consider was whether I still loved Hew. Analyzing this was like trying to hold water in my fingers: it could not be grasped and could not be broken down into less-slippery components.

I thought of the day we'd met. Hew was then on the Cornell IT desk and I had needed someone to salvage the hard drive of a laptop that I had, while wandering in a state of high focus, accidentally dropped down a stairwell. When he was done, a sticky note on my new computer's desktop had Hew's name and number. I texted him because I was, by this point in my first year in Ithaca, desperate to get laid and did not, at this early stage at my new university, want the person who laid me to be someone I knew through physics channels. I had the idea—I admitted this to Hew only after we moved in together—of finding a sexual routine that would not distract me too much from my work. But soon I found myself wanting more of Hew in my life than planned. He was an unassuming and, for this reason, highly effective advocate for himself. He was a little goofy, very sharp, judgmental but always sly about it. Soon his voice was living in my head with me. Soon we were together every night and it was hard to imagine the time when we hadn't been.

Anyway, I was now attempting to imagine the counterfactual. My Excel re Hew reached 377 rows. This was small compared to where things ended up. Every positive seemed offset with some ancillary negative, which was in turn offset by some further ancillary positive, and so on and so forth.

I did not realize for a few days that I was trying, in effect, to simulate the entire remainder of my life. When I did realize this, I thought: Why not? The Hew model became significantly more complicated after I determined that some effects were mutually exclusive, and that nearly all effects affected the likelihood and intensity of the others in some way, which meant I had to revise the model to assess the likelihood and intensity of each outcome in light of all the other outcomes. This took almost four days and only after I was done did I understand that I had basically re-created a chess computer, like Deep Blue, only the problem was less bounded and thus a lot more complicated than chess. The game tree as I had designed it—Helen versus Life—would require *significant* scientific advances in quantum computing before any machine could give me an answer.

In other words, HTS was a fairly simple phenomenon relative to what I was now attempting to simulate.

And speaking of HTS...

Even in retrospect it is hard for me to believe I did what I did. How could I have thought I would get away with it? If I was being irrationally hyperrational re Hew, my logic re Perry was reptilian. I had become so immersed in solving for Hew that I had not, for several weeks now, done any meaningful revision of the HTS model. Of course I'd imagined I could catch up—a few all-nighters and I would be back in the game! So I had been telling Perry that the work was in progress and on pace, don't worry your pretty little enormous bald head.

Meanwhile the model remained in the same state of disarray it had been in before Christmas, when I'd stormed from Perry's house and, in so doing, surely diminished a bit further whatever already-diminishing confidence he had in me.

Two days before my deadline, panic finally set in. Suddenly I remembered what an extraordinary thing it was to work with Perry. He trusted almost no one to do the work I did with him. But I knew my status must now be perilously close to "everyone else" in his book, which is to say I was starting to appear useless, or at least more trouble than I was worth. Probably I would never be as much of a dud as Devlin, that type, but I could see myself fading into yet another bright Smoot student who had not quite blossomed. For twenty years Perry had been searching for the person who could help him solve HTS; I was the latest try, and if I could not get it together, I would not be the last.

I knew I had to find some way of reestablishing his confidence in me. What I lacked was the will to actually do my job. The day before we were scheduled to take control of the supercomputer, Perry emailed to confirm that everything was ready to go. I said, You betcha.

That night I stayed up, trying to cram more than four weeks of work into sixteen hours.

Then time was up and, against all reason, or maybe with the sole reason of buying myself a little more time, I uploaded the model to the supercomputer and hit play.

33.

A couple of weeks passed. In the basement, 522 petaflops whirred with my useless code. What I was doing in the meantime was approximately as useless. I ought to have scoured the latest literature in search of some sky-cracking insight that would compel Perry to abort the current version of the model in favor of a new one, yet to be written. But superconductivity still couldn't hold a charge for me. I was not indifferent to what would happen with Perry but I was, perhaps, resigned.

What would happen with Hew—*that* felt urgent. The Hew model was hilariously infeasible, but I could not stop working on it. It gave me an excuse to avoid Hew himself, and Lens too. I fiddled endlessly with every value and probability. I re- and re-reorganized the logic. Coders call this gold-plating; it felt productive and cathartic, almost profound. All the more so in my case because no hardware on earth had the power to produce an answer. The model provided a structure for and visible map of the issues. It assured me I was thinking rationally. Of course nothing could be more arbitrary or less rational than assigning a weighted longitudinal life-enjoyment value to the presence or absence of another person's scent compared to another hypothetical partner's scent, but there was also no apparent more-rational approach, so I continued toggling as the HTS model ran and ran—and finally ran down.

For one thing, it finished six days earlier than I'd thought it would. This was not a sign of overachievement. It did, however, give me a chance to look through the outputs before Perry knew we had them—and the results were not good. I had botched the very first line of code, our boundary conditions, which I had left open instead of changing to periodic. Very embarrassing. For reasons of computational feasibility, HTS models must use an atomic lattice of artificially finite size, like a rectangle cut out of chain link fence, and you have to decide how to model atoms at the edges that do not connect to other atoms on all sides. For process reasons it's best, while drafting, to assume the lattice just ends: boundary conditions open. But for precise results you have to close the boundaries before you run the simulation, which means linking atoms on your right edge to atoms on your left edge, so that electrons flow out one edge and back in the opposite edge—like Pac-Man. I had forgotten to write in these periodic boundary conditions, and as a result the edges of our lattice glowed, very obviously, with artificially trapped electrons.

In addition I had not correctly tracked single- and double-precision variables through the model, and there were hundreds of instances of summing single- and double-precision variables, which completely defeats the point of using double precision at all, and this was why the model had finished so much earlier than expected and why its results were much less precise than Perry had explicitly demanded.

In addition I had made an off-by-one error when switching between Fortran and C++, which in layman's terms means that I had started counting from 0 when I should have started counting from 1, and in practical terms meant that this highly iterated subroutine I had learned an entire new programming language in order to write had produced several million incorrect inputs, distorting the entire simulation into physical nonsense.

These were errors for which there was, at my level, no excuse. Certainly there was no excuse for making all of them at once.

It was February, and the weather at RIP had entered a phase of unrelenting shittiness. Constant cold wind and freezing, swirling, angular rain. I longed for snow, something I could defend against.

The walk to Perry's house felt grim and shameful. Other people, I know, spend a lot of their academic careers in this fashion; taking tests unprepared, submitting papers drafted overnight, riddled with typos and light plagiarism. But unpreparedness was new to me, in the academic dominion at least. There was a difference between the types of mistakes I usually made and what I was about to have to own. I was not and until now had never been a *lazy* person. I was often wrong but always, until now, meticulously so. What I had done with this simulation was so sloppy: that was what most bothered me and what I knew would bother Perry.

When I rang the bell I was thinking that my best shot to win Perry to my side would be if I owned up and told him the truth: that I had been distracted because Hew intended to leave me, and that my mental bandwidth had been devoted to *that* problem.

At any rate, the whole issue was moot.

Perry's door was answered not by Perry or Williams but by Devlin.

Helen! He beamed. He embraced me. It is *so* nice to see you. It's been *too long* and now *here we are* on Plymouth Island! Can you believe it?

I said: Hi.

Devlin watched me shed my boots, then led me to the living room. He poured coffee from a glass carafe on a side table. He was as tan, as glowing as ever. He explained that Perry was on a phone call, could he get me anything to eat?

Devlin's tone, like the whole vibe at Perry's, was highly domestic, cozy in defiance of the weather.

He settled onto the sofa and beamed up at me.

Obviously, I thought, I have missed something major. It goes to show how our preoccupations consume us that I did not even nearly guess what was happening. My initial suspicions followed this convoluted chain: [1] Perry had noticed my sloppy work. [2] He had therefore brought Devlin in to replace me. [3] Therefore I was presently the victim of a coup. However, if this was the story, [4]

Devlin must be significantly cleverer at coding than I ever gave him credit for? Could I have written Devlin off too early, and incorrectly? Because [5] maybe *that* explains why Perry would ruin his own life, and mine, over Devlin?

I asked, What are you doing here? I felt pranked. I waited for a camera crew to emerge.

Better for Perry to explain, said Devlin. But really I just *can't* get over how *happy* I am that we are both here. I've kind of missed you, H. We *must* take a photo for the others. Devlin stood, put us in a selfie, and sent it to Edward, Ming, Ivan, Xiao Xi, and Omer, with whom we'd started graduate school almost six years prior.

Okay, well, what are you doing these days? I asked. Devlin had finished his degree and last I heard was working for Citibank. Perhaps he'd found this as uninspiring as it sounded to me. Perhaps Perry had arranged a postdoc for him at the Institute?

But Devlin said: Citibank! Enthusiastically. I am still getting used to the money. I still eat *ramen* half the time! He clutched my arm and went bug-eyed, like Can you believe it?! But I think I *will* get used to the money, ha ha ha ha ha.

I hear, he said, that you have been doing fabulous work.

Perry said that?

Who else?

When did he say that?

He says it all the time! He won't shut up about how amazing you are. It's infuriating.

I thought: All the time?? How often can these two be talking?

Fascinating, I said. He does not say it to me.

Come on, we don't need any of that. Devlin flapped his hand as if wafting away an odor. False modesty doesn't suit you, my dear. How's your dad?

Now, I had to smile at this. Devlin and my dad had met precisely once, when we were presenting our master's papers, but they had hit it off in such extreme and unusual fashion that Devlin asking after Dad became a kind of joke. Dad had said more to Devlin during one dinner than he'd said to me in perhaps six months, aggregated. They'd been like gossipy housewives, Dad as energized as I'd ever seen him.

Dad's doing great, I said. He always asks about you.

Does he *really*?

No, dear.

You wench. Don't get my hopes up like that. What's his lady's name again?

Patricia.

Patricia, Devlin said, with faux loathing.

Where is Perry? I'm glad to see you but I would *really* like to understand what is happening here.

So far the evidence was not fitting well with my theory that Devlin wanted my job. Devlin could be bitchy, but I was not getting even a whiff of meanness from him. He seemed too genuine, too enthusiastic. Plus what he'd said about getting used to money from Citibank indicated that he intended to keep getting used to it, right?

I had seen Devlin just a few times between Perry's dismissal and Devlin's graduation. I had not, in that period of flailing failure, been feeling especially social. And I'm sure I harbored some impolitic, unspeakable animosity toward Devlin for what he had let Perry do to him and then for what he had done to Perry, and to me, in return. So Devlin and I had never discussed Perry post-cancellation. Devlin had talked to the *New York Times* but he did not allow the subject to consume his life. He had not talked about it with anyone, as far as I knew. I never learned materially more details than had been published in the paper.

This despite the fact, as I was now recalling, that Devlin and I had been *friends,* hadn't we? Devlin was acting so familiar, and at first I'd thought he was exaggerating, overcompensating. But actually it was pretty bizarre, now that I thought about it, that Devlin and I had not talked in any meaningful way for over a year. Early on in grad school we'd all had dinner—Devlin, Hew, and me—almost weekly. I imagined that we had drifted apart, gradually separated like wheat from chaff in the physics grind, as daily patterns changed and life intervened, etc. But had I actually *abandoned* Devlin? Had I dropped him not gradually but instantly, when it became clear that I would have to choose a side in the divorce of Perry from Cornell? I remembered—shame drove me to remember—how Devlin had texted right around when Perry told me what was going on; Devlin had texted to see if I was up for a drink, maybe Thursday or Friday?, and I had not responded for weeks.

Devlin, in any event, did not seem to harbor any hard feelings. He was pouring more coffee and telling me about his apartment in the West Village.

Finally Perry emerged from his office.

Look at this! he said. All three of us together. It is almost as if I'd never fled Ithaca in disgrace!

Devlin said, I have been holding Helen in *terrible* suspense. You must explain the situation.

Ah, well. I was hoping you might have done it.

That honor is yours, Perry.

For god's sake, I said.

Perry remained standing but squared up, facing me. He was fighting a grin. Some part of him couldn't wait to tell me whatever he was about to tell me. He said, The incident with Devlin... was arranged.

Arranged?

Planned.

By Devlin, I said.

By myself, primarily, with Devlin's assistance. It was fabricated *on my behalf.*

Perry looked at me as if I were now meant to infer the rest.

I said, You will have to lay it out for me, Perry.

I *wished* to transfer to the Institute. But B.W. Rubin, if you would believe it, would not hire me! He thought I was ideologically misaligned, too woke or something. He would not take me! So I determined I needed some skin in the game. I realized I needed, rather like entering a *gang,* to commit some offense that would initiate me.

It took some time, Perry continued, to come up with the right thing. I did not, of course, want to do anything truly coercive. I thought about publishing something asinine and offensive, but I was not sure B.W. would believe that. Then Devlin here rather *presented* himself to me.

We've always been close, gay alliance and all that. But then I tried to kiss him, said Devlin. I suppose you'd say I started it.

Perry said: Devlin believed he was seducing me when I *reversed* him with an immodest proposal. We would *manu-facture* an affair, a falling-out, and some impropriety from myself over text message and email. In the end Devlin would turn me in and I would confess to having done these horrible things that I did not in fact do, thereby securing the position I wanted here at the Institute. It was fanciful and I did not, in truth, expect him to agree. But he did. It was . . . It was an extraordinary thing for him to do for me, putting himself out in public as my survivor.

Oh, Perry, hush. I didn't mind.

Perry seemed a little choked up, actually, talking about Devlin's sacrifice. Your reputation, your career—

We all know I did not have a future in physics. I was never going to be like you or Helen. I didn't lose a single step, professionally. And if you think being the spurned lover and bravely outspoken survivor of a Nobel laureate has hurt my social prospects in New York City, you have misunderstood the culture, Perry.

Anyway, Perry said, we made it up. There you have it.

You know, Helen, last time you were at the house, I was here too, actually, said Devlin. We had intended to tell you then, but Perry got cold feet.

I did *not* get *cold feet.* I didn't want to distract her. It wasn't the right time.

Perry made me hide in the bedroom with Williams! I was *ordered* not to come out to see you!

They both looked at me with these bashful smirks. They thought they had just let me in on a juicy hunk of gossip, like I would be delighted to finally be in the know, like I was now a co-conspirator...

Maybe I would have felt that way if their scheme hadn't upended my entire fucking life? I was facing *divorce* because of this Institute! RIP had been an intellectual disaster. I was perpetually swatting away or hiding from unwanted attention, and, far more obtrusive, I was suffocating under the stupid, all-consuming controversy of living here. This Institute had commandeered and derailed my life of science, *my life of the fucking mind*—not to mention potential progress toward room-temperature superconductivity that could literally *save humanity's future on earth*! And it turned out Perry had done this *on purpose*?!!?

I would have liked to witness whatever was happening on my face that caused what was happening on theirs. Their grins dissolved. Their eyes went narrow and anxious. They realized they were watching a fuse burn down.

The ensuing explosion went along the lines of: Are you *kidding* me? Was there a single spinning fucking muon of your being that cared what this would do to me?

Perry said that he had *of course* considered what would happen to me, which was why he had from the outset secured a graduate position for me at RIP. He said he had been surprised I was so hesitant to come, that he had thought me above or at least *external* to what he dubbed "irrelevant woke bullshit." He said: Truly I'm surprised at how much the Institute seems to have thrown you off! Your recent work has been subpar, as we both well know, Helen. This last version of the simulation is a mess.

You looked.

I did.

Ah. Well...it's bad, I know. But I have been preoccupied with figuring out how to prevent Hew from leaving me.

I'm very sorry to hear that. You know you could have asked for more time.

You know, I bet you're *delighted,* Perry. Soon I won't have any life at all distracting me from being your code monkey, your math mule. You'll have me all to yourself. I'll spend thirty years as a nun for physics and then maybe one day I too will try to seduce a goddamned undergrad.

All right, Helen.

If Hew leaves me, that now goes on your side of the ledger, Perry. Along with everything else this year. Fuck.

All right, Helen.

Perry was placating me. I felt childish and hysterical, felt the high ground slipping away, though undoubtedly it should have been mine forever.

I'm going, I said. I need to talk to Hew about this, damn your secret, and he is probably going to want us to leave immediately. Do you have any problem with that?

Please, Perry said, I hope you won't leave. But if you want to tell Hew what I did to get to the Institute? Go ahead. You and he are probably the last to know it.

On the way back to the Endowment, I was a bullet through the rain; I was livid and impermeable. Suddenly it was all so obvious: the extent to which Perry had adopted the Institute ethos; that *duh* look Lens had given when I mentioned how much Perry seemed to like it at RIP. This glance had been nagging at me for months. It was one of the only times that I had sensed Lens withholding. Perhaps Perry had told Lens? More likely, I thought, Perry was a type. Probably he was not the only person here who'd actively wished for the freedom and luxury the Institute promised—and then had to manufacture some way to deserve it. Which left me with a self-pitying question, a question addressable only to gods and therapists, of which I had neither: What had *I* done to deserve it?

34.

I said, Aren't you going to say something? Aren't you going to ask if I'm mad enough that we can get away from this place?

Hew said, Are you?

Maybe.

Let me know if you make up your mind. His face held a taut, depressed grimace.

Can we—Can you please just—? I'm upset. Here, I said, and grabbed his hand, and for a while we just sat on our sofa, looking out at the water. I put my head against his lean, bony shoulder.

I think we should stay, he said later.

Maybe that should have been enough to cause me to overtly query ulterior motives. Maybe this was the moment for me to ask whether the other person he obviously wanted to stay near was Melissa or someone else. But it is funny how things become unmentionable between two people, how the most logical idea becomes unthinkable.

You lose trust in another person and find you can't trust yourself anymore either.

All I said was: *You* want to stay?

I just don't see what's changed.

Well, Perry lied to me, to us. It's all been . . . a manipulation. That's a change.

Hew said: We thought Perry had done something bad, something abusive, and still we agreed to follow him. Turns out it's a different offense from what we thought. Devlin's not the victim; we are. But we followed him because you wanted to keep working with Perry on HTS. And you can still do that. And it *is* still important. You know I know that, right? I believe what you once said to me was: Yes Perry is a schmuck and he put us in a bad spot but for god's sake have a little perspective.

Cheap, I said.

But not wrong.

Suppose I said: Let's start packing.

I mean, we both know how this ends, Hew said. I don't know if you'll forgive Perry but I already know you will keep working with him. Of course you will. You are seeking something. Perry can help you find it, and that's all that will matter in the end. This drive you have, this relentlessness—I've never been able to compete with it, and that's because you can't compete with it either.

It threw my whole breakup model off-kilter, hearing this. Statements like these were a specialty of Hew's. He had this way of dropping totally accepting yet candid yet resonant descriptions of me into random conversations. They decimated any chance of quantifying what he meant in my life. For a moment the constant fog of human loneliness would clear and I would feel so profoundly *recognized,* so honestly but also fondly characterized, and Hew was the only person who'd ever made me feel like this.

Maybe I *could* give it up. There are other things I could do. I smirked. There's always the National Security Agency.

Oh *Christ,* Hew said. And I thought the *Institute* would be the peak of villainy in our lives. Why is it, do you think, that such a high proportion of the employers who seek strong math skills are so nefarious? Finance, tech, the NSA...

You have a theory—so tell me.

They all need to get away with something.

And math helps—?

Because they need to outrun and befuddle the rest of us. Only a few of you have the math to actually understand what's going on, everything they're doing. So if they can *employ* all of you they're home free. The rest of us will either pretend to understand or won't even try, and either way they can do whatever they want.

Do I befuddle you?

Daily, Hew said. I think he meant this warmly but in fact he seemed exhausted.

He said, That's why I like this dynamic equity thing. Using math for real good.

Right, I said, though I had no idea what he was talking about.

That was a pretty good night for Hew and me, the best we'd had in months. I thought maybe peace was at hand?

We curled into each other, his long chin nesting in my big hair, maintaining touch as we slept all the way into the morning. And not long after, I understood why we had finally broken through, why goodwill and compromise now reigned between us. The stakes were vanishing. Hew had still been trying, in his own way, but now he was giving up. Or maybe I was.

35.

Perry and I had not spoken for about a week.

Well, yes, I knew, said Lens. And I had a pretty good guess that you didn't.

You have no problem with it? I said.

I wish I'd thought of it. I might even use the idea. What a nice plot.

A plot against *me,* Leo.

Oh, hardly. He thought it was for your own good. If there is a victim, I think it's B.W. and therefore who cares?

Why—I gulped and reset. Why will no one get on my level about this? Not you, not even Hew. I've been lied to, betrayed, manipulated! I've been *used.*

Sure. But has it hurt you?

The kettle whistled and Lens, standing above it, promptly removed it from the heat and filled the glass teapot. I paced on the kitchen island's opposite shore, noting Lens's olive knit sports coat, the surprising fullness of his shoulders, the way his thick gray hair splashed out and around his forehead. His eyes caught the reflection of the snow-dusted field beyond the window. They tracked me lightly, playfully, flirtatiously or perhaps condescendingly.

This Institute is—It's like I'm being slowly poisoned. I don't think you've ever *met* me, Leo. That is how thoroughly unlike myself I've been. I'm terrible at my job. Hew intends to leave me. I've been disrupted, and the disruption, I now know, traces back to Perry's blasé, idiotic assumption that I would have no problem whatever uprooting my whole life to follow him to the most provocative zip code in the United States.

But *why* aren't you able to work? I am as much a prima donna about my working conditions as anyone, but I have no problem working here. Lens's tone was diagnostic. I felt him prodding my brain, simultaneously therapizing and gathering material.

The problem is—the problem is fucking *politics*. Controversy. You can't eat a meal in one of B.W.'s gourmet dining halls, you can't take a walk around this opulent campus, without constant prickling reminders of the ideology and the money behind this place. The men here are like goldfish rising to the top of the bowl, mouths open; I have to wear headphones everywhere. And even when I can get some peace and quiet there is no such thing as peace and quiet here. We are at the epicenter of this unrelenting barrage of criticism, debate, news, political *foam*. It all used to be irrelevant to me. But now the Knights of Right talk about the Institute, so Hew and I have to talk about the Knights, about the Institute, about how we *feel*. It's inhuman not to. But it's exhausting. And really not interesting or intellectually profitable, as far as I can tell. Why must politics always be the main thing? We are meant to be in a haven from so-called woke oppression but actually the constant controversy here is more taxing than wokeness ever was. I cannot tell you how thoroughly nonpolitical my life was before. I was *all* science. Politics was trivial to me; it was *decorative*.

Well, of course you were nonpolitical, Lens said. You were living under tyranny! You do not need politics under tyranny. Politics is distracting, frustrating—and yes, oppressive. But it is the price of a free mind.

I did not ask what he meant but before I knew it Lens was talking about the Soviet Union. This kind of thing happened with Dad too. It felt like having a stroke. You thought you were in the middle of a comprehensible, logical conversation and then suddenly found yourself midlecture in a course on Isaac Babel or the Great Terror. Lens said something about someone named Yakov Sverdlov.

I said, What on earth are you talking about?

My point is the Bolsheviks were *just* like you. They too thought that politics was suffering. In the heaven they were trying to achieve there would be no politics; controversy would vanish into an objectively correct consensus of the one, good way to live. In their vision, eventually there would be no government, yes? And so no room for debate or further modification of the rules. In *this* country, we understand—or at least we *used* to understand—that everything we choose to do is temporary, imperfect, subject to revision. *That* is the heart of liberalism. Judaism too.

For us, the stakes are not *so* high. We try and try to make things better; maybe we win, maybe we lose, but always we know there will be another game, and another, and another—forever if we are good stewards of the system. That is why we don't have to kill each other over every little thing.

But if you are trying to *end* politics, he went on, you do not think that way. The stakes were much higher for the world's Sverdlovs. Just think: a Jew standing over the Romanovs with a pistol, a Jew sending his own family to the labor camps! It is because he was a *Bolshevik* before he was a Jew. They thought they were fighting over terms that would govern humanity finally and for all time. Naturally, if you believe that, any violence, any extreme, is not just permissible; it is necessary. It is the same with all of these millennial cults. Severe Christians, radical Islamists, and earnest Communists are exactly the same in this way. Your cohort, as I've said, so aptly named, millennials. They're just the same too. It's why they were so glad, at first, to exile us to this Institute.

I said, Well, the politics of living here is as authoritarian as any dictator. So if my life presently is what it is like to have a *free mind,* the Bolshevik millennials are onto something.

But, you see, it is not B.W.'s *ideology,* the Institute's ideology, that is the problem. You feel the *subject* of politics rules you. You are the *subject's* subject . . .

He was talking to himself, basically. After a moment he said, And so you are. We all are, probably. Lens said this with objective finality, as if he had finished some mental arithmetic, and finally sat in the armchair above which he'd been hovering.

I went to the bookcases. My fingers traced the worn spines of 1970s editions of Dostoyevsky. Lens had arranged his books by nationality; these shelves held Russians. British literature and American literature were to my left, other world literatures to my right. I felt Lens's gaze on my back—on my legs, on my butt.

Well, I said, I guess—why exactly shouldn't I prefer the bubble? In the old bubble I could think about scientific problems that humans might actually solve, instead of interminably debating ancient and intractable disputes of values. Why shouldn't I put my limited mental capacity into something productive? Why would anyone *want* me to spend my energy developing the "right" opinions? I'm not the President. My opinions are useless—to me most of all. I can *work* inside the millennial consensus, so what's wrong with wanting it back?

The democrat in me would say you would be missing out on so much life, you would be missing out on understanding and learning and the full range of liberty that is your right. But I know your rejoinder.

Which is?

You will say, Lens said, smiling, You will say that I, Helen, am a world-class racehorse, and you do not let a world-class racehorse wander about to nibble at meadows and meet other interesting, different kinds of horses. With a world-class racehorse you tightly control its environment and its diet; you train it intensely and sensitively. Only if you shape its surroundings to let it focus singularly on running does it have a shot at the Triple Crown.

I was laughing. I said, *Uncannily* like me, that analogy. As if from the horse's mouth.

Lens stood and went toward the kitchen, then stopped in the threshold, turning to me. I have some advice, if you'd like to hear it, he said. You really may decline. I know how sensitive women of your cohort can be to advice from a fellow of my age.

Leo, you just gave a Cold War sermon on Bolshevik ideology. The line that you don't want to cross? ... It's behind you.

I'll go on then.

And I'll listen with equanimity.

So there is one obvious thing to do, an easy thing. And then there's an alternative, much more difficult. The obvious thing—Lens spread his arms—is to really, finally embrace this place.

He stood there, grinning; I felt his invitation in my chest.

The water is fine. There must be some part of you— and surely there is some part of Hew, tall white fellow that he is—that *yearns* for the eternal sunshine of the un-woke mind. Just think how *beautiful* it would be to wake up and be yourselves—smart, educated, lucky, white, straight, American people—without feeling like your very existence is traumatizing untold numbers of people you've never even met. You probably call this conservatism, I know, but it's really just liberalism and capitalism and a simple hypothesis that the best rule is to ignore groups and treat every person like an individual, full stop. Not too long ago these were not totally outlandish ideas. They were *progressive* values, in fact. You can *embrace* them and set aside all this religious guilt. Just something to consider.

Yeah, I'll, uh, bring that proposal to my board of directors. But now I'm dying to know, if that's the *easy* path, do tell what's the hard path?

If you can't embrace this place, turn it into fuel, Lens said. This *frustration* you have: remember it is *fuel* if you want it to be. I know you know this. I mean only to remind you. Maybe people are delicate about a racehorse. But the racehorse itself, the racehorse itself is not delicate. It is fierce, it is ruthless, it is single-minded. It knows its purpose. Its whole world is fuel. Do you understand?

I let the subject drop. With his every incantation of "fuel," the word had grown weightier, more mystical. The invitation in his voice had become a kind of dare.

His gray brows glared fiercely at me. In his furious gaze I saw all his betrayals and sacrifices, all the family love and sentimental attachment and professional camaraderie that he had denied himself in the extremist pursuit of his art. What I might have said if it would not so obviously have upset him—if it would not have upset *us*—was that I had just identified the way in which even he, Leo Lens, was a Bolshevik.

36.

There is no such thing as a stable disequilibrium, nor a world without entropy—but sometimes you can persuade yourself. For a while I was able to take as an operating premise that everything was or would naturally become fine. Or at least I could believe that whatever was not fine was in my head only.

Tentatively, Perry and I reopened diplomatic relations. I made changes to our code, fixing the things I'd botched. He sent me a list of new ideas. HTS—Hew had predicted it—required our attention. Perry and I stayed together for the kid. For a while we communicated solely through notes in our code in GitHub, asynchronous messages in the cloud.

Through my revisions, I tried to make clear that I was, after a long mental hiatus, finally back at work.

One impetus to refocus was, obviously, Hew. I could no longer stand to deliberate about him, about what I knew was coming, so I had to engage my mind elsewhere.

The other impetus was that Perry and I suddenly had serious competition. Through an unassuming post on the *Science* blog, we learned that Zhou's team, the MIT team, the Institute for Advanced Study team, even UCLA had all abruptly pivoted to neural-network-assisted HTS strategies. They would be channeling a constant flow of experimental data into AI, finding new ways of asking the *AI* to find the pattern, rather than finding it themselves.

Why had everyone else done this? Were they onto some new algorithm? Had their ability to train a neural network finally caught up to the complexity of superconductivity data sets? Back when I first started real physics, I'd been amazed at the extent to which the skill base of scientific discovery was not actually about mastering theory but about maximizing the capabilities of technologically limited tools. The challenge was to draw the greatest possible insight from humanity's fairly rudimentary telescopes, microscopes, sensors, and computers. Once you are past classical physics and into quantum phenomena like HTS, existing tools are *really* rudimentary. A good analogy is that folk parable: blind man, place your hand upon this elephant, now describe the whole creature.

So I wondered about a breakthrough in neural networks. About three years ago I had suggested to Perry that we could try one. This provoked a smoldering diatribe about how the only reason one would want AI to identify the pattern is if we do not think humans will be able to cognize the relevant principles, and if humans cannot understand it *what is the point of making a machine "understand" it*? Science *progresses* only when the underlying principles of our world become *simpler, more fundamental.* The concepts get more abstract and harder to grasp, perhaps, but the formulae become mathematically *simpler.* If we cannot express our discovery on the side of a tote bag, we have *failed,* etc. etc.

Perry persuaded me. In any case an AI pivot was a nonstarter on his watch. The only other choice was to redouble our efforts.

Maybe I was also learning to take Lens's advice re fuel? It did not work for me quite the way Lens suggested it might: the trend toward chaos in my life, the ceaseless political maelstrom, my seemingly impenetrable uncertainty on all matters of moral significance, these were not themselves fuel as I suspected they were for Lens. But the feeling they created in me—the sense that something drastic must change or something dire would occur—this absolutely was.

Anyway I caught up on the latest papers, the latest data. In one interesting paper, experimentalists at UC Santa Barbara had achieved superconductivity at 57°F (!!!) by bringing a novel hydrogen compound, a photochemically transformed carbonaceous sulfur hydride system, up to pressure of around 2.6 million atmospheres (!!!). In layman's terms the new, promising compound was basically flatulence, a freeze-dried fart. Of course the message boards burst with commentary: We had the answer within us all along! Room-temp superconductivity was right under our noses!

But the unexpected success of this hydride system meant Perry and I could confidently implement some changes in our model; decisions about disorder and the stability of a carbonic lattice were no longer guesswork to quite the same degree. From here the adjustments cascaded. One day I figured out a mechanism for memory management— keeping every one of our double-precision variables in RAM (fast) instead of hard-disk (slow)—that would cut our run time by eighty percent. It was the smartest thing I'd done in a year at least. I reported it to Perry like a child reporting an A+.

Pretty soon I was wandering, unwashed, through the Endowment's basement hallways. I lay, cogitating, on the floor of the server room, wedges humming and flickering around me like stars; in my mind I'd already rendered them obsolete. I dialogued with myself during meals, on the toilet, reorganizing, compressing and simplifying.

Hew, too, was withdrawn, phone bound, otherwise occupied. I wondered what he was waiting for—if he even knew what he was waiting for. Probably we were both swinging toward some aphelion, perhaps graduation or our next move or our next big fight, when our orbit might most naturally break.

Occasionally, for instance when I was waiting on debugging, I would go into my model of life with/without Hew and disable its more sophisticated and computationally infeasible components, and then in the simpler version I would toggle this or that parameter, watching what happened to the Total Divorce Value. But the model was glitchy. Among the problems the simplified Hew model had was that I could no longer get it to output a positive TDV. Somewhere I had made an error. However much I exaggerated and biased the inputs, the TDV approached 0 asymptotically but never crossed above it.

In other words, there was no world, the model thought, in which it was preferable for Hew to leave. This, I thought, this *cannot* be right.

37.

Finally the newest model was as robust and de-tailed as Perry preferred—and taking that level of detail as a premise, I did not think it could be made more efficient or capture more atoms. I had proofed it ten times. Of course we'd been here before. You could never reasonably hope that *this* version would finally capture the phenom-enon, blow the whole problem wide open, but neither of us could think what else to do. We needed to productively fail again before we could see a path forward. Unquestion-ably what we'd built was state of the art. The memory management optimization I'd used was publishable in its own right. And if the results were coherent, it would be the best science I, or anyone, could do at the moment to improve on the old ZEST and BCS models.

Perry and I sat side by side in lab. We had by now seen each other in person several times since his great Devlin disclosure, but I'd stopped inviting myself to his bungalow. Weeks of relative peace in my life made me determined, here on in, to rigorously maintain ordinary workplace expectations and boundaries. I attempted a policy of détente. I thought if I remained dormant, passive, perhaps the tension that had been mounting between me and every significant man in my life—Hew, Perry, Dad, Lens—would dissipate and resolve.

Beyond unusually clever math, the model we would soon run featured a real physical insight courtesy of yours truly. I'd realized that vibrations in the atomic lattice were more likely to transfer between layers in carbonaceous systems in a very specific way and that there was a mathematically plausible representation of this principle that actually *simplified* the phenomenon of HTS and, accordingly, our model, such that we could perform exact diagonalization on as many as 280 atoms!! My idea was what physicists like to call an ansatz, a pretty good guess. Certainly good enough to try. If it proved out even in limited circumstances, it would get us a paper in *Nature* and support my eventual tenure file.

To properly test the idea, however, would require culling about 2,443 lines of just-polished code. It meant more delay. No change would be permanent if it failed, but still, I could not implement such a change without Perry's *ex ante* agreement. So I had asked him to meet me in an empty classroom. I pitched the principle and the math.

He said: Okay.

I kvelled. It was a lot of trust to put in me, and a deferral of his own ideas. More credit than the usual graduate student gets.

So for the first time in months I was really appreciating

Perry, felt affirmatively glad about working for him—and Perry, to his credit, I think enjoyed seeing me strut. *Finally,* it felt to me, I had assumed command of our project's general strategy instead of dutifully drafting beautiful code to his specs. We both sensed that I, however circuitously and unexpectedly, had reached another level of physical vision. Perhaps I had been borderline incompetent for the last few months not because I'd had too *much* responsibility but too little? My new role suited me and, for the time being, suited Perry.

So we were both in a fine mood, sitting there in lab, sifting for bugs one last time in a model that had now become *mine* as much as his. I would never have brought the subject up ever again when Perry said: I realize I owe you an explanation.

I told myself I didn't want to hear it—Who cares?? Who *cares* what trivial strife inspires the selfish decisions of selfish men??—except I really did.

The explanation: I was unhappy, Helen. I would not have expected you to see it. I did not want anyone to see it. To be in my position in the world and be as unhappy as I was—it felt absurd; it felt *unrealistic*. I had accomplished so much more than any man has a right to. I had a worthy life's work. I had students, like you, that others would kill for. How could a man in my position be dissatisfied? So for about thirty years I did not quite believe it myself. But in the end, this unhappiness was happening to *me*. I saw how much of my life had passed. I could not ignore it any longer.

In a way it is easiest to guess the problem if you know

nothing about me except what anyone on the sidewalk could discern. Look at me, Helen. Try to see what is actually salient: the physical form. I have never transcended this body, its physical properties. This body *repels* love, physical affection. And for most of my life I went without. Not an absolute famine, but closer to that than I would like to admit.

It is a law not of physics, I suppose, but of human nature: The body sets the terms. It declares how easy or difficult everything else will be. People *do* sometimes overcome their bodies, of course. And I might have done that too, if it had not been for my personality.

There is only one environment in which I am *comfortable,* in which I understand and can perform the appointed role. That is why I so rarely venture beyond the university town, the academic campus or conference. I am deliberately provincial. I have *no* life beyond the life you have seen: working, teaching, entertaining my students and colleagues. It is all I am cut out for.

The rest of the culture, the "adult" world...it is difficult for me. It is too *laissez-faire.* The social aspect, I mean— how does one simply *meet* someone? And what does one talk about, how does one discover what one must learn about another person, if one cannot talk about physics or at least departmental politics? I'm stifled, suffocated, when I'm outside of academia and can't talk about my work, when I can't appropriately attempt to *educate* the person I am talking to. Of course you know only what it is like for me *in* the water. On a campus I am at ease and naturalistic, or at least I feel that way. On a campus, I make sense.

All of this is to explain why, after many years, I came to understand that I had no hope of finding love, of finding intimacy with which I was comfortable, outside the academic setting. More precisely . . . more precisely, I knew that the only relationship in which I would be myself had to be inextricable from the rest of my identity. I needed a romantic connection in which I remained a scholar, an educator. That is *who I am*. Alas, I came to know this about myself just as the academy decided that such relationships were to be entirely verboten.

For years I hoped for a change—in myself, in our society, either would do. I hoped the pendulum would swing back and that they would lift the "administrative policies" they had imposed on relations between full professors and students or junior colleagues. I waited, able to believe for a while that this puritanical turn in the culture would pass. Surely I was excusing my own cowardice, too. These policies provided me with an explanation, a pretext, for how lonely I had become. I was a good citizen; this was my sacrifice. When society came back around, when it realized its error, *then* I would finally be happy, and in the meantime I had my work.

And the error. My god, what a *fundamental* error. These lines they've drawn, policing the subtleties of human relations: It is wrong on an *a priori* level. I can say this to you, technically my student, only because of where we presently sit, at this Institute. But I will say it. There is something erotic that is *inherent* in true education, in true intellectual engagement. I know you feel it for me as I do for you. It's why Hew and I are jealous of each other. You

and I are connected; we are *attached*. Intellectual attachments and emotional attachments and erotic attachments
are all made of the same particles. There is no rigorous
way of distinguishing among them, and to build an entire
regulatory scheme on this wishful *lie* . . .

To demand that I should form meaningful connections
with my students while abiding such *artificial* limits on
those connections . . .

I ran out of patience for it. I wanted clarity. It *could not
be* that virtuous living was all a matter of adhering to other
people's ever-shifting sense of proportion. If the current
rules made sense to anyone, they did not make sense to
me. My university position, my credentials, my Prize—
the world assumed these things made me *powerful,* but I
have never been powerful, Helen. Not a day in my life.
Not in matters of Eros. Who could know that better than
I? So I was not the person everyone had decided I must be,
and I was nonetheless living by rules aimed at constraining
completely different types of people, and meanwhile my
time on this planet was slipping away . . .

I *mean,* Perry said—as if in silence I'd argued an
opposing position—what could be *more* erotic, really, than
the relation of teacher and student? I am not a pederast;
it is not about youth *qua* youth. It is about the flow
of knowledge from one person to another, that thrilling
awakening—discovering the world and one's place in it.
Of course it is about power, too, control and submission,
master and apprentice. Other lovers build scaffolding to
simulate these dynamics. Subs and doms, role-play. In the
educator-educated dynamic, you have it all right there, the

real roles, organic. Why shouldn't I be able, if I am decent up to my *own* standards, to allow this one vanishingly narrow area in which I *am* a quote "powerful" or attractive person to commingle with and help me in the romantic area of life, in which I'm otherwise helpless? Musicians do it, and actors, and the wealthy. Everyone, I thought, except me.

Ask yourself why, given how attached I believe you and I are to each other, why is there so little *sexual* charge between us? There are the obvious obstacles: my sexuality, my body. You love another person. But look deeper. I have had some other female students toward whom I did not feel quite so *inert*. The reason there can be nothing between us is that we are too evenly matched, too equal—for my taste anyway. You are my student only nominally, by the happenstance that you were born a few decades after me. In terms of your ability, your rigor, your vision... There are one or two people, emerging perhaps every five or ten years, who are like you or me. I hope you know that if I ever talk down to you that is a mistake on my part, a habit of tone that is hard to break. But we are peers, basically. You are thus not at all my type.

Then take someone like Williams, on the other hand. With him I am and will forever be in the position of his elder, his teacher. We have the necessary imbalance. Without that imbalance I am both helpless and invulnerable; I am immune to intimacy. But what is another word for imbalance? *Charge.* The charge with someone like Williams lets me receive gifts that the world does not otherwise give me, and I can, at the same time, manifest my best qualities: my warmth, my humor, my ability to make the world cognizable, to guide and to give away what I have learned.

I *did not fit* with the world back there. He gestured vaguely west, at the mainland and Cornell. As soon as it came into existence, I knew this Institute could offer me a chance to be as I really am. That it would free me to find someone like Williams, to be *aboveboard* about the whole thing. *Here* I would not be such a misfit. Honesty, and happiness, might be permitted for me.

You can see, can't you, that it was at least reasonable for me to want to come here? And you can see too, I hope, why I might have been...a bit myopic in assuming that you would not mind. The mainland academic ethos had so thoroughly failed me that I thought it must be failing everyone, whether or not they admitted it, including you. I know now I was wrong. I suppose the mainland served you pretty well. At the very least you were accustomed to it, you had chosen it, and I ripped you away. That was unfair of me, Helen. I was inconsiderate, and I am sorry.

Perry waited a polite ten or twenty seconds to see if I had any response. I did not. For five minutes I'd been staring at my feet. There were so many possible, counter-vailing reactions; they did not exactly cancel each other out so much as they required processing, computation time. I said: Okay. Let's do this.

I hit enter, and three floors beneath us 522 petaflops went to work.

Probably I would have said a little more to Perry if I'd known this would be the last time I ever saw him.

38.

On March 18, 1987, a few thousand members of the American Physical Society stayed up all night at the New York Hilton Midtown. They crammed into sweltering ballrooms, sat cross-legged on hallway floors. News of the impromptu event had spread by word of mouth, at first. There had been no time to go to the printer, so the signs announcing the papers, the speakers, the schedule, this way to the overflow room, had all been written in Sharpie.

Embedded among the physicists: about a dozen bewildered Hilton employees, distributing coffee, cookies, finger sandwiches; dealing with the trash. These physics men—it was about ninety-five percent men—kept telling the staff that it was all very exciting, that they were about to witness history. Hi-T-C, Hi-T-C. This phrase the staff kept hearing—was it a word, two words, an abbreviation?—was indecipherable even after one of the physicists, already on his third cup of coffee and the panel

213

hadn't even started, tried to explain it. It had something to do with ceramics. The jittery physicist swept nine cookies off a plate and held the plate up saying, This! It could be a *super*conductor! The whole *world* is about to *change*.

The distinctly hippie vibe in how he said this accurately represented the heady optimism of the American Physical Society circa 1987. What was about to commence would become known, adorably, as the Woodstock of Physics.

The event's abruptness and late hour owed to a blitz of discoveries, as recent as the prior weekend, showing that some unknown set of exotic materials, the key properties of which were also unknown, defied the classical linear correlation between temperature and electrical resistance. Almost anything will superconduct below a certain "critical temperature" just above absolute zero and then stop superconducting as soon as the temperature increases above that, with resistance to electrical current increasing roughly in proportion with temperature. Then, at IBM Zürich, Georg Bednorz and Alex Müller discover, after hours, on borrowed equipment, a lanthanum-based cuprate perovskite that exhibits the Meissner effect—the expulsion of a magnetic field that occurs when a material transitions to a superconducting state—at a temperature of 35 degrees Kelvin. The University of Tokyo replicates their result. Paul Chu at Houston then tries YBaCuO, which becomes the first compound known to superconduct above the temperature of liquid nitrogen. All of this should have been impossible. Now that it was known to be possible, all knew the explanation lay within the enticing black box of quantum mechanics.

The excitement in that room, I would posit, owed not only to the new fact of high-temp superconductors. I would argue that perhaps the more important thing, that night, was the uncertainty in the air, the fact that no one on the planet understood what they were witnessing. Uncertainty meant possibility, potential.

These discoveries had all happened in the space of a few months, too late for the standard submission deadline for APS, and the breakneck pace of new discovery had everyone picturing a ladder dropping down from the physics gods: right this way to your next transistor, your next electricity. In eighteen months, maybe two or three years, it was assumed we would have mastered the physics of high-T_c superconductivity. Sometime shortly thereafter, mass availability of inexpensive superconducting materials would give us a lossless electrical grid; the Meissner effect would give us hovering, frictionless trains. Probably cars, if not pigs, would soon fly.

Woodstock turned out to be a good analogy, because the optimism of that night at the Hilton did not quite pan out. Nearly forty years later, Perry and I and a few thousand others would still be working the basic science of HTS. But that HTS would take so long to grasp was as unfathomable in the discovery-drunk atmosphere of APS 1987 as the possibility of HTS had been unfathomable at APS 1986.

That night, at the on-the-fly high-T_c superconductivity session, fifty-one (!!) papers were presented between 7:30 p.m. and 3:15 a.m. The sunken- and wild-eyed physicists then hung around until 7 a.m., discussing everything they had just heard, reliving it. The Hilton's other guests, visiting lawyers and management consultants in crisp suits, emerged from the elevators and scanned the lobby, puzzled, then went to attend to the business of Midtown.

Over time, public memory of that night distilled to a few iconic moments. Hendrix's "Star-Spangled Banner" was the perfectly curt, suppressed Germanness of Professor Müller announcing that a superconducting film had been developed "over the weekend." All recalled the joyous cheers when Bertram Batlogg of Bell Labs, overwhelmed as he tried to arrange data on the projector, brushed his graphs aside and declared: "I think our lives have changed." And no one could forget what became known as the Fifty-Second Paper.

The Fifty-Second Paper story was told repeatedly at Perry's memorial service. It was far from Perry's largest scientific contribution but it was probably the most theatrical moment of his career and it seemed to have defined the way many of his peers thought of him. It had been like going to a high school basketball game and there's this guy playing, what's his name? LeBron? If you knew anything about the game you were agog.

A young and then-unknown Perry had waited in line, in the crowded aisle, for nearly two hours to ask a question. He was prominent even before he spoke because of his physical size and because, unlike the other physicists, all reduced to sweaty shirtsleeves, the dandyish Perry remained fully suited, pocket square and all, in a beautiful soft herringbone jacket with the volume of a hot-air balloon.

It was around 2 a.m. when he got his turn. On the grainy video of the event, you can't see and can barely hear Perry, but you can see the faces of the people listening to him. They accept a scrap of paper and, looking down at it, start nodding, astonished.

On the paper was a list of indium-based materials that Perry guessed they had probably tried and that had not worked, i.e., had not superconducted except at a temperature of near zero. These guesses were correct in the sense that many of these materials had indeed been tried, and the rest were all soon ruled out as HTS candidates. Perry explained from the aisle that the atomic lattice in this subset of indium-based cuprates would probably not be rigid enough, above 20ish degrees Kelvin, to allow consistent Cooper pairing. Also on Perry's scrap of paper, soon copied onto a transparent slide for display to the whole room, was a sketch of a few different indium-based atomic structures, with weak bonds labeled to illustrate the theoretical basis for his prediction.

To those who were not too fatigued to follow, it was immediately clear that this rotund twentysomething was very likely correct, and that he had probably just saved physics writ large the trouble of trying a few thousand indium variations one by one.

It was also clear that he had figured this out *in the room*. Of the fifty-one papers presented, most were not yet published. So Perry could not have read more than a few in advance. He had been among two thousand other physicists and, just sitting there, assimilating the data and diagrams, had discerned a minor theoretical principle of

HTS and applied it for immediate scientific profit. Someone would have discovered the indium problem eventually, after enough experimental failures, but to get it so *quickly*, to get it when indium compounds had been mentioned only once or twice in the last five hours... He had been looking at the negative space, pondering what hadn't worked while everyone else talked about what had.

Even the very German Müller had been so excited by Perry's diagram that he could be heard above the shouting, saying to Paul Chu: Mein Gott! I vasted almost *sree months* on indium!

So by the time the lawyers emerged for Continental breakfast in the Hilton lobby, everyone at APS had heard of this young guy Perry Smoot, who soon had his first paper in *Science*.

The memorial service was in Columbus, Perry's hometown. The city was not easy to associate with him. If there was anything extreme about Columbus, it was very extreme normalcy. It was an exceptionally standard place, a Platonic American form: standard beige downtown anchored with a few large companies, state government, a state university. It had a standard hip neighborhood, standard wealthy fringes, standard slums, a standard galleria. Perry's family, also normal: two sisters, both high school teachers like Perry's parents had been, and a sprawl of Midwestern cousins, nieces, nephews. How had *Perry* emerge from this? He had driven the Columbus public schools to surrender and was allowed by reluctant parents to attend Phillips Andover on scholarship, and there had bloomed into the great flamboyant genius.

In Columbus, everything about Perry seemed normal except Perry himself. Even his death. There'd been no drama to it. He went to bed, suffered sudden cardiac arrest, never woke. For a man of his age and size, whose diet consisted primarily of pâté and ACE inhibitors, it was actuarially punctual. This was four days after I'd last seen him, and a few hours after his last email to me, diagnosing some peculiarities in the midcalc summary statistics we'd been getting from the ongoing simulation.

The service was held in a brick Colonial-style mansion that had been donated to the city and preserved as part of a park. The walls crawled with creamy floral moldings; the floors held an old dark stain, traffic-worn to a light tan in every doorway. The native Buckeye elements of Perry's life did not seem to know what to make of the academic contingent and vice versa. I was surprised— even Cornell's dean had showed up. Apparently Perry was nontoxic now that he was dead? I wore a navy dress and black heels. I ate a mushroom tart and handed one to Hew.

I had been unable to persuade Hew that I really preferred to go to Columbus alone. He claimed he had his own, personal respects to pay, and it could not be denied that Perry Smoot had, through me, played a large role in Hew's life over the last five years. Nonetheless, his insistence seemed absurd and even invasive to me— that he would attend against my will after being so em- phatically *against* Perry and encouraging me to desert him! What I really thought, in that week's dark mood, was that Hew had demanded to come along in order to deny me any accusation of neglect when he soon announced his departure. This is inorganic behavior, I thought, these are "virtuous" acts in anticipation of litigation.

Hew and I stood listening to another account of the Fifty-Second Paper. He didn't have to say a word for me to know what he was thinking. All made worse by the fact that so far, at the service, Hew had not said a single unsupportive word. He was behaving flawlessly. He kept giving my hand affectionate squeezes that I kept shaking off. I just didn't believe him. My attention was elsewhere, or wanted to be.

Eight Nobelists attended, and others who were destined one day to win it—all of these people Perry's friends and colleagues from a long and social career. The glaring absence, or at least glaring to me, was Lens. Did I really think he owed it to Perry to be here—or did I just want to see him? Lens had been radio silent for over a month, and I'd been stewing on the possibility that this was purposeful on his part.

Anyway the full extent of Perry's socialness surprised me. With everyone in the same room it felt like those early photos of Earth from space; finally you could see the complete picture of the system you were part of, the pale blue dot, the Perry galaxy. Like all great masses, he had spent his life drawing people in, giving direction. The energy that Perry had not spent on romance, I thought, had gone into this. He'd made himself patriarch and mentor to hundreds in the scientific world. He'd kept in touch.

And for this reason everyone seemed to know of me. I was *the one* who went with him. You were his favorite,

Perry's sister whispered to me. Perry hoarded you, one quantum theorist said.

The physicists kept offering help, giving me their phone numbers and emails.

This, I suspected, because I was transparently fucked, career-wise.

I *dreaded* trying to analyze the results of our latest simulation without Perry. For a week I'd been thinking that if there were a leper colony, a max-security penitentiary, another island of violent sex offenders, where I could go to continue working with Perry, I would do it. Suddenly the Institute felt like a small price to have paid.

In the last week I'd been back on Google Translate to exchange short notes with Zhou, who'd shared the Nobel with Perry. I'd hoped to see Zhou at the funeral but he said, I am regret cannot arrive America. He was a victim of his own success in more than the usual way: ZEST, the Prize, was probably the worst thing that ever happened to him. Since then he'd been under surveillance, no longer permitted to leave China for fear he might defect. Still, I was thinking that perhaps I should go to Chongqing; I'd try Mandarin again, it cannot be *that* difficult if a billion people speak it; and wouldn't most of my work with Zhou be in the universal language of code?

Hew took my hand again. An experimental particle physicist was telling a story about Perry. They had never previously met nor worked together but one day Perry had called and, without prologue besides announcing This is Perry Smoot, instructed the experimentalist to bombard barium atoms with two identical lasers to determine whether the photons ever scattered into an odd number of fermions or whether they were firmly bosons, which would help validate a key assumption underlying Bose-Einstein statistics and Lorentz invariance. Before the experimentalist could ask Perry why he was gifting this idea—instead of doing the experiment himself—Perry hung up. Later he learned that Perry had seen one of his minor papers and decided that the experimentalist was reasonably rigorous, did not write scientific puffery, already possessed quality lasers, and had so far been floundering on an unrewarding path of study.

Of course the experimentalist performed Perry's proposed experiment, earning a paper in *Physical Review Letters* and opening a new lane of inquiry in which this experimentalist, whom Perry had impulsively deputized, was now the grand pooh-bah, a pioneer, and the recipient of disproportionate grant funding.

Everyone agreed this was just like Perry, giving away a perfectly good idea like that. He had been brimming with them; he had too much inspiration to use it all himself. What would it have taken for Perry to personally set up this giveaway experiment? Not much. He could have teamed up with a seasoned experimentalist down the hall and shared the glory of the final paper. Instead he gave a stranger a career.

Isn't that perfect? Perry in a nutshell? I said to Hew.

Perry in a nutshell. That's an image.

He was kind of a prince, wasn't he?

Hew said, Let's not get carried away.

After the reception, as we were walking into our hotel, Hew was looking at his phone and said, Oh Jesus.

What?

They're not charging him. From Thanksgiving, that rapist. The grand jury wouldn't indict.

Oh, I said.

... Is that all you have to say?

I shrugged.

He said, No one is going to do anything about this guy. No one. He will keep his luxurious job; he will keep *teach*ing. No tangible consequences for him at all. And you say Oh?

Fine, you're right, I'll get started on a position paper just as soon as we finish my mentor's funeral.

You don't need a goddamned position paper. You just need a regular human emotional reaction. For god's sake why not just have the totally *obvious* reaction? Is it really so complicated?

It's an injustice. It's wrong. You want me to rend my garments?

You're unbelievable, Hew said. For a while he lay on the hotel bed, ankles crossed, smoldering down into his phone and typing madly.

I mean, I really don't get it, Helen. How is it that you have such *empathy,* such enormous reserves of understanding for Perry Smoot and Leopold Lens—but for this girl you can't muster more than a syllable?

And something in me broke down. I said: Why are you calling her that? "This girl."

What?

You know her. Melissa. I've seen you together. Why are you calling her "this girl"?

Hew squinted through his glasses. What are you talking about?

I saw you and Melissa together, in the lobby, in December. She's the one you're always sending those disappearing messages to, right?

What? No—no. I met her, once. We were waiting for the elevator. I told her I believed her and that I was sorry. I don't know her. Apparently she won't even leave her dorm anymore.

Okay.

Do you think I've been *seeing* her? The look on Hew's face: the bafflement, the rage. The sense that he had been entirely misapprehended. That *I* had entirely misapprehended *him* . . .

No, I said, not really.

Who do you think I am?

We haven't been right, Hew. We've been off for a while, and I saw you with her and for a moment I thought—I don't know.

Oh my god, obviously we're off because of where we have to live. Because I'm *angry* all the fucking time. And sometimes I don't know who I am or who the hell you are.

It's been a long day. Can we just leave all this alone?

No, no, we can't, he said. Not this time. The problem is it's always too easy to leave these things alone. Almost everyone at that service today thought Perry exploited one of his graduate students. But how many times was

Devlin mentioned? Zero. There were one or two oblique references to what Perry did, or to what everyone thinks he did, and then ah, never mind. The rest of the day was this celebration! How could that *be*? How could Perry's greatest sin, or at least the greatest sin we know of, end up so unimportant to how everyone remembers him? Because that's what's going to happen with Melissa too. Already she's being brushed aside, and when they eulogize the supposedly great scholar who raped her, I guarantee no one will want to think too much about her—her suffering, this girl, this sophomore studying Henry James, who just wanted to feel *smart*. Not everyone is so sure they are smart, Helen, like you are. Is it really so fucking hard for you to grasp what life is like for most people? Melissa—she just wanted to feel like a good writer and a good student. She wanted just a *taste* of the approval that you have spent your whole life swimming in. And this is what she gets? For wanting a fucking *internship*?

By the end of this Hew was shouting. His long arms flailed almost to the ceiling, his suit jacket flapped, his glasses rattled on his nose.

I was so exhausted. If I had been wrong once I didn't care if I was wrong again. I said: Look, Perry was a genius. Objectively. Must the bad thing always be the main thing? What Perry gave to science, to the world. . .this sounds crass but it *is* more important than the rest of it, isn't it? I know it doesn't go for everyone. I'm not saying that when you bury Charles Manson you'd highlight his lovely singing voice. But for Perry—physics *is* the main thing. . .it drowns the rest of it out. Why can't that be the answer?

You cannot mean that.

I think I do.

And Roman Polanski is a great filmmaker??

Among other things, isn't he?

Physics is the most important thing *to you,* Helen. *I* don't give a shit. Whatever the purportedly bigger picture might be for you, whoever Perry might have helped or been kind to, whatever his academic import—I've seen none of it. The entire picture from where I stand is a selfish bulldozer of a man with regressive politics who spent his last months on earth molesting an undergraduate and who has, infuriatingly, subjected my life partner to Stockholm syndrome.

This is a life sentence? I sighed.

When, Hew asked, are you going to see that we have to be *ruthless* about these people?

But why can't I miss Perry too? Why can't I admire him too? When are you going to admit that the right thing to do, the full moral measure of a person, is not always that goddamned simple?

Except sometimes, it is. Sometimes it is very *very* clear. I am so tired of being embarrassed, with perpetually apologizing for the five percent of men who are causing ninety-five percent of the damage. Why do we keep squinting to see the good in them? We'll find ourselves some *new* geniuses who know how to behave. These people need to feel our *wrath* when they abuse their strength, their power, their luck. And make no mistake: Perry did that. He did it to *you* and to *me*. I've been watching in *astonishment* as you go from rightly irate at him, to accommodating, to forgiving, and today positively sappy about him.

He's dead, Hew. And *you* told me to stay.

I told you to stay because I knew you would. And— And I regret it, honestly. *What the fuck has been happening?* he said. There were tears and a kind of wild extremist fervor in Hew's eyes. It was disgust, contempt, visceral. Directed at me, I thought then. I thought that he was not planning to leave me for someone else; it was worse. He was just leaving. I had repulsed him.

Though of course I understood this conversation differently after Hew went to prison. There was no way I could have known what we were really talking about.

The last thing Hew said before I took my jacket and left the room was: We can't chalk every piece of abuse up to some immutable quota of worldly injustice. We can't just *forgive* these pricks, Helen. We just *can't*.

39.

I went to the lobby bar and wept a little. I ordered a pulled pork sandwich.

I worked over some rebuttals to Hew along the lines of glass houses, buddy; remember you were not always so sure you were above reproach yourself; remember you're not always so selfless yourself; remember that you yourself need forgiveness every now and then you sanctimonious smug goddamned blah blah blah.

While I ate the first meat I'd had in ~8 months I kept thinking about an old Argonne Lab paper, one of those flash-in-the-pan discoveries that looked for a few minutes like a breakthrough but then nothing had come of it. The paper showed that the transition temperature of lanthanum barium copper oxide actually went *up* when you corrupted the sample with impurities, probably because increasing disorder suppressed the charge density waves, a conclusion they had corroborated with X-ray scattering at Cornell. There had been something about this idea nagging at me for months, like Perry and I were not properly accounting for it in our physical model, but I'd never mentioned the issue because I could never quite identify it. It was one of about a hundred ideas I'd had in the last week that made me long for Perry's help. Anyway finally maybe I was putting my finger on it...

Then I thought: Holy Jesus Crap Myself Christ.

I was pretty sure I had just solved high-temperature superconductivity.

40.

To Professor Engelmeyer-Lipschitz at
Stanford, I wrote:

Dear Professor Engelmeyer-Lipschitz,

Thank you for your kind offer of help when we met at Perry's memorial service last weekend. I do have something I'd like to ask. I am trying to wrap up some work Perry and I were doing together. It would be helpful to know the transition temperature of an 80% pure sample of $YbMgGaO_4$. Could you have someone run that experiment and send me the results?
Thank you for considering this strange request.

Regards,
Helen

I sent similar letters to Professors Davis, Chou, Finzi-Severini, Calvin, Thorpe, Rojas, and Steinberg, the differences among the letters being the materials to be tested. To a person, the professors said it was a fine and appropriate commemoration to do one last experiment at the suggestion of Perry Smoot; it was the least they could give to the man who'd given so many insights over the years; they would see to it these experiments were promptly done...

The rest of it I had to do myself. I was starting from almost zero. Only fragments of what Perry and I had been doing the last five years remained relevant.

This turned out to be no problem because I entered another plane, coding-wise. What I was building was immensely complicated, but I moved through it with enchanted confidence. To say I was in the zone does not remotely communicate—I was in a state of *supernatural* situational awareness. I was pirouetting between raindrops, seeing the whole vast board. Devilish traps and pitfalls and false doors fell untouched behind me. What it felt like was stepping off a cliff and finding a new path rising up to meet your feet, then that thrill repeated constantly for days and days and days until you are sure that you can do no wrong, that something transcendent flows through you.

For the rest of my life since then, I have been chasing whatever I tapped into. It was actual perfection. I can guess at the conditions that made it possible—grief and dread and excitement and an *idea*. These were all present in extreme volumes that cannot be artificially synthesized. Emotionally I was an exposed nerve who had somehow wired herself into the fabric of the universe, with my fingers at the other end, emitting code. All I had done for this discovery was to add <1% of insight beyond well-established ZEST, a nudge beyond what had already been hypothesized. Why was I the one to do it? Luck favors the prepared and desperate mind, I suppose, and that is all I can honestly say. It came to me.

The final model was sufficiently lean that you could run it overnight on a laptop if you wanted the transition temperature of only one substance. But I didn't want to go substance by substance *seriatim*. I was so confident that I wanted to simulate 100 materials at once, so I ran it on the supercomputer. It took a while to input the atomic structures for 100 substances, but then when the model ran at 522 petaflops the whole calculation took slightly less than a day. There was no suspense. I knew it would work.

The end result was a Persian rug: gorgeously intricate, coherent data that showed, for 100 forms of hard condensed matter, the pressure, disorder, temperature, and etc. at which it would transition to a superconducting state. The model's predictive power was enormous. It would turn the search for a room-temp superconductor into a monthslong computing exercise, rather than the decadeslong Iditarod of difficult, expensive physical experiments on which physics was presently embarked.

Professors Englemeyer-Lipschitz, Davis, Chou, Finzi-Severini, Calvin, Thorpe, Rojas, and Steinberg had each gotten back to me in the meantime and their results fit my predictions. I had needed them to do these experiments because there had not been, up to that point, a lot of systematic testing on the role of disorder, i.e., impurity, in candidate high-temp superconductors. Or if there had been such testing the results were not published. Scientists

are constantly disserving one another in this way. Everyone declines to publish their bland failures—there is no
professional angle in it—which thereby ensures that many
other scientists will experience the same bland failures
firsthand.

Probably I'd *over*proved it. Even without the Engelmeyer-
Lipschitz, Davis, Chou, Finzi-Severini, Calvin, Thorpe,
Rojas, and Steinberg results my predictions would have
been undeniable. The model lined up flush with all of the
high-quality published experimental data I had selected at
random. Add to that the new results from Perry's friends,
the variance in disorder I had distributed among these
unsuspecting preeminent research assistants, and I could
now explain roughly why my model worked to an eighth
grader.

Yes, I thought, this could fit on a tote bag.

One thing you learned early and then tried to get over,
if you chose to pursue physics, was that many physical
laws are bursting with symbolism. Entropy, for instance, or
gravity, or magnetism. These concepts are *dying* to become
metaphors. You want them to be *meta*physical laws, to say
something deep about human relations. You had to get
over this instinct to analogize at every turn because it was
too hacky, too obvious.

Nonetheless, as I paced around the Endowment basement, not quite believing what I had done, I thought
there was something profound in the physical principle
I had just demonstrated. I was very tired, it should be
said. I tend to become grandiose when exhausted. I was
thinking that it had to mean something that *disorder* had

been the key. Ideologically it was very Perry, very Lens. In HTS models, you had to include a disorder parameter to account for impurity—for, say, the stray zinc atoms where copper should be in a sample of bismuth strontium calcium copper oxide. No real-world substances are entirely pure. But disorder was a pest; it was assumed it could only interfere with HTS, not enable it. For decades, materials science had been twisting itself in knots trying to synthesize simple, pure samples—materials we believed we could test and model and understand. But then disorder, the impurity, this *messiness* had actually been the answer. There was *something* significant to be learned, I thought, from the fact we had spent decades squeezing out the very factor that would have gotten us better data, a better grasp of the phenomenon, closer to the truth.

Also I thought it had to *mean* something that my breakthrough had been so similar to Perry's Fifty-Second Paper. Like him, I'd found the pattern by looking at the negative space, the failures, the candidate materials that hadn't panned out. Perhaps I would never have thought to do it if he had not died, and then if I had not gone to Columbus, where everyone kept talking about Perry at the Woodstock of Physics, and who knows maybe if I had not fought with Hew and been so mad that I ate meat—if I had not had illicit pork in my system while I thought about disorder in Columbus, Ohio—maybe it would never have happened. Some mystical forces had aligned. Briefly I entertained the possibility that Perry's spirit had inhabited me.

Another mystically prescient thing, not identifiably mystical or prescient except in retrospect, was that I declined to tell anyone what I'd done. There was no natural outlet, I suppose. Hew and I had barely talked since Columbus. Lens remained incommunicado aside from a short condolence note, delivered to my apartment atop a robot cart, after the news about Perry reached him. Plus I liked that for now, for just a little while, this knowledge would be mine alone. I could enjoy the achievement without the distortion of compliments and envy. For a little while, I was the sole human being in all of history who understood the basic quantum principles of high-temperature superconductivity, the one person who really *knew* that the world was about to change.

I left the Endowment and began, without any destination, to walk. On the path I passed a couple of red-pilled US historians who had together been ejected from Amherst. Across the blustery quad the former governor of New York shouted into his cell phone. I walked through town, where the former CFO of General Electric entered the bar where he led a twice-weekly support group for men in recovery from insider trading. In the restaurant next door, a famously corpulent professor emeritus of the Princeton philosophy department dined with her young mistress.

I boarded the ferry to New Haven. I was not quite sure what I had in mind until I stepped off the boat and got past the protesters. From there I went to a Korean spa I had seen several times from the road.

I was almost the only white person there, and this felt correct. I was in strange territory; I had appropriated some knowledge that I was not sure I was entitled to.

For six hours I had my hair straightened, was manicured

and pedicured and scrubbed rosy with pumice and salt. I was acutely massaged, seaweed-wrapped, steamed and baked. I lay on hot rocks, then cold rocks, then warm rocks, then I steamed and baked again. I meandered around a great tile beach, dipping in hot, warm, and polar pools, bathing in the chatter of nude Korean women. What I'd wanted was an environment as foreign and serene as I presently, briefly, felt.

41.

It worked, didn't it? B.W. was not really asking. He knew. Somehow.

I had arrived back from New Haven on the last ferry and, in the Endowment lobby, had been swiftly approached by a pencil-skirted middle-aged woman who said that B.W. would like to see me, she would escort me up. I had demurred, telling her, truthfully, that I had not slept in about forty hours and could only technically be considered conscious.

The next evening the pencil-skirted woman rapped on our apartment door, requesting again that I please go upstairs. Hew glared. I still had not told him what I'd accomplished.

Probably to spite Hew, I said Fine.

The woman did not speak on the way up and wordlessly held the elevator door for me at B.W.'s penthouse. Then she departed.

I entered the great room: the Rothko, the Japanese cricket

cages, the unicorn tapestry from the Cloisters. At the far wall, above an eighteenth-century Spanish credenza, B.W. poured scotch. There was no one else. Oceanic twilight lit the ceiling, which slanted upward toward the panoramic windows. The room felt like a mouth that wanted to eat the world.

You've done it, B.W. said. I knew you would. He replaced the bottle on the bar and walked over to me, holding two glasses, winding his way around Rodin's bronze bust of Napoleon.

What do you think I did?

I thought: *How did he find out?* And so quickly?? Maybe it had been a mistake to use the supercomputer. Its logs were public and one day's unscheduled use might have triggered his suspicions. The even more perturbing alternative was that he not only persistently surveilled my laptop but also had someone in his employ who could understand the code I'd written, which would mean there was another very good numericist essentially living inside my brain.

Of course B.W. had no intention of telling me how he knew what he knew. The mystery of his omniscience gave him more authority than any particular explanation.

It's extraordinary, Helen. Drink this.

I don't like scotch.

You will.

The arrogance of the rich. I sipped and still did not like scotch.

We should discuss your future, he said. He led us toward two long, low, modernist leather sofas that were facing each other across a black marble-block coffee table. But he remained standing, so I did too. You'll have your degree, of course. I mean after that. What sort of arrangement would suit you?

I intend to leave, I said.

He sipped.

He said, Wouldn't you like to hear my offer? It's the best you'll get.

I am pretty likely to win the Nobel Prize, I said. After that I expect fairly good offers.

Well, you see, whether you win a Nobel Prize is up to me. Whether anyone knows what you've done—that is up to me. B.W. broke eye contact and wandered away, around the back of the sofa, pretending to examine some ancient Chinese calligraphy on the wall.

Your work occurred on my premises, on my time, on my equipment. The legal stuff is in the forms you signed when you joined the Institute. To the greatest extent possible, I do believe in academic freedom, the culture of public knowledge and all that. But in this case I fear it's not possible. You've done something too valuable. To become the world's sole supplier of room-temperature superconductors... It would be financial malpractice to allow you to publish.

He still was not looking at me. I stiffened and placed my tumbler on the coffee table. I said, Are you really not rich enough?

He turned and stared at me, from a distance of perhaps twenty feet. You've probably heard this before, he said. It's a cliché because it's true among people like myself: It's not the money itself, but what the money *represents*.

You and I may have different views on what the money represents.

I worried we might. So I've locked your lab and your cloud access, and I'll be holding on to your laptop until we reach an agreement.

What?

I'll tell you my offer. His tone was impossibly neutral. His left hand held his scotch and his right hand emerged from his pocket and began to count off the points he was making, starting with his thumb.

You'll have your own lab, more funding than you could ever need, and complete exploratory discretion. You will also supervise a small army of materials scientists perfecting our superconductors and ancillary technologies built with our superconductors. You will be the chief scientific officer of what will shortly be the single most essential and most innovative component supplier on the planet. And if all goes well, I will allow you to publish—*not* the whole model, of course, that will remain a trade secret in perpetuity—but once we have any necessary patents I will allow you to publish your discovery of a few particular room-temperature superconductors. I'm confident that will suffice for a Nobel Prize, if you must have one. I have some influence with the Committee.

Now, he said, the other option is that you leave without a degree and under a strict injunction never to tell anyone, in any form, about the work you did here. If you tell anyone you'll be so enmeshed in lawsuits that you will never have another moment for physics for the rest of your life, I guarantee it.

I felt nauseated. It was hard to say whether this owed to the substance of his "offer" or whether it was because, as he spoke, B.W. had approached and somehow meanwhile held his scotch extremely still. From three feet away, with only the coffee table between us, his face remained both an inscrutable smudge of wealth and intensely, vividly ugly, weak featured, open-pored.

Sit, he said. And I sat.

He took the opposite sofa, facing me. He leaned forward and put his elbows on his knees. His tone softened.

Look, he said. Strictly speaking, I don't need you to use that amazing model you built. I *want* you to stay because of what you may do next. I have an eye for excellence, Helen. I sensed what you were capable of accomplishing from the beginning, even before we met, from the way Perry described you. I thought you might need five or ten years to do it, and I was prepared to retain you for that long. You cracked it in months. Just extraordinary. I can't tell you how it *invigorates* me to be around a *woman* of your ability.

He wasn't large but somehow he loomed. His *will* loomed.

B.W., it's—it's just wrong, I said.

It was like I'd said nothing. No flicker of pause or hesitation.

We will make an exceptional partnership, Helen.

When I watched B.W. stand up, I was not thinking about why he was standing. I was thinking about litigation. I was thinking about spending decades in a state of grievance and defensiveness, decades during which I would be under fierce scrutiny, decades with no room for error. I was thinking about my dad's clients, about divorces I'd witnessed, the way legal disputes absorbed attention more totally than even politics could.

When B.W. sat on the couch beside me, I was thinking about what it would mean to have an enemy. To have *him* as an enemy in an asymmetrical war. He, so lavishly resourced he would be unconcerned with the costs of lawyers or even the probability of victory. And I, without funds, fighting for my life, for my scientific and personal reputation, which I had surely already compromised by coming to RIP in the first place.

When B.W. adjusted his slacks and crossed his legs toward me, I was thinking about how I could not, at present, prove to anyone that this discovery was mine.

When he put his arm across the back of the sofa, I was thinking about how I did not know what was in the con-tract I'd signed, how I did not know the law—whether he could really *own* my model? Whether he could really stop me from publishing or how he could punish me if I did? I was thinking about how I did not know everything a person like him could do to me, how I did not know what was at stake.

He shifted closer; his hand lay beside my throat. Now I finally knew what I was feeling. Power.

What do we mean when we say we are a free country? I think it means that if you go through life moderately independent, not unusually strong, capable enough, you do not often find yourself on the pointy end of power. Of course you are submitting all the time to the powers that be: to law, to physical and financial reality, to the preferences of family and friends and colleagues. That is the inherent compromise of living in the world; that is every person's lack of omnipotence. This is in contrast to acute power, the ability of one person to block all the exits and dominate you. Suddenly I had no doubt this was what B.W. wanted—it's what the sex *represents*—and for the moment I saw no way to stop him.

I don't know. In retrospect I suppose I still had exits. One problem was there was not a lot of time to think. Another was that I had no experience with this. For so many reasons—my brains, my weirdness, my man-repelling default style, whatever—I had previously drawn a few creeps but never an assault. Very good fortune for any woman. Or at least, and what a mindfuck, or at least it feels that way until you find yourself unprepared, lacking the tools that you'd like to imagine would have gotten you out of there, and for a while afterward you are furious with the whole educational establishment for having failed to provide *courses,* maybe some trial assaults, *some* kind of *training* for when one of the world's wealthiest men holds your life's work, your career, and the entire planet's future hostage and now leans all the way in.

B.W.'s face was inches from mine. In the mirror behind him, I could see the tapestry of that beleaguered medieval unicorn.

For several endless seconds I waited for him to touch me. I almost wish he had. Then at least I would know for sure whether I would have let him. Or whether I would have recoiled, pushed back, fled.

He inhaled and then exhaled, slowly. I felt his breath in my hair; I smelled his immense self-restraint.

·B.W. stood up. Think it over, he said.

He took his phone from his pocket and looked down into it.

You can go, he said.

So I went.

42.

For a while it was impossible to tell Hew, so instead I went after Lens.

Even as I was obeying it, I wondered about the evolutionary basis for this instinct to roll your shit downhill. Someone does something wrong to you and you decide you have not merely a right but actually some kind of responsibility to pass the wrongness along. Maybe you do this because you think that if you *distribute* the wrongness among enough people the burden on each person will be bearable, whereas one person bearing the aggregated weight is very much not. Of course the math doesn't work out because wrongness is cumulative; it compounds more easily than it divides; still—

Lens had not wanted to let me in, but I imposed myself. From his stiffly pocketed hands, his furrowed glare, the absence of an immediate offer of tea, I could tell I'd interrupted writing. He kept glancing away to his rolltop desk, as if ideas were crawling around in there that might escape.

I said, Make us some tea, would you?

He filled the kettle. Is something the matter?

I followed him into the kitchen.

Well, you've been avoiding me.

I'm avoiding everyone. I'm mid-siege.

I don't think that's the reason.

How was Perry's service?

Fine, Leo.

How was the attendance? It may herald attendance at mine.

People came. With one notable exception.

He scowled. Have you come here for an argument?

Not an argument, no.

All right, I'll venture a guess: What's going on with you and Hew?

We're hardly speaking. That's getting to be normal.

Lens looked at me, an invitation to elaborate. I silently defied him.

How long did you know Perry? I asked.

As an acquaintance? Perhaps a decade. As a friend, just recently, since he arrived here. People my age do not make many new friends. So it was a treat. *He* was a treat.

Well, it was a good fit.

Sure, it was . . . But I want to know how you mean it.

He was your Bloom, your Ravelstein.

Yes.

Bellow probably attended that funeral, don't you think?

He did, and so did I.

Now Lens smirked defiantly. He was not going to apologize or explain himself. We glowered at each other across the kitchen island. Certainly in this state of animosity, I had no chance of seducing him, but I was not turning back. I intended to brute-force the problem, to exert my will directly, and thereby either succeed or find my limits. I channeled B.W. Rubin.

I thought: This man has had hundreds of women. Hundreds of women have had him. This is someone who is *susceptible* to women; he can be coaxed or, failing that, overpowered. It is in his *nature* to do what I want.

I leaned over the island and put my hand on Lens's. I looked him dead in the eye and said, I want to fuck you, Leo.

He looked me dead in the eye and said, We are never going to do that.

Is there someone else you prefer?

That is not the issue.

Have you lost the capacity?

In a sense, he said.

What he meant was that he had given up intentional destruction. He explained it all very succinctly, in what sounded like practiced remarks. He had been avoiding me, yes. Because he'd sensed my desire to go further, do more, be reckless—and his own desire for the same. He too had felt that stirring in the air between us, the feeling that in another world, another life. . . . But he was done following his nose in that direction. It always caused conflict, was often a mistake. The kind of hurt that would inevitably accrue to Hew and to me and to Lens himself—for Lens now such drama belonged only in his work. He'd had enough of having his way; he'd had his turn—more than his turn—at wreckage, at overthrowing life. He would do whatever damage he wanted in and with his work, as always—and the price, he'd decided, was that he would otherwise behave well. I find you alluring, yes, he said, so I was avoiding you. To the extent I know I cannot control myself, I must control my environment.

Intentional destruction was precisely what I at that moment most wanted, so I was livid, hearing this.

I said, What I think you mean is that you can't get it up.

He twinkled at an impending joke. His expression was eerie, right out of Dad's repertoire.

Lens said, I would prefer not to.

43.

Who knows what made Hew go through with it. Maybe if things had not been quite so frigid between us. Maybe if Melissa had gotten justice. Maybe if she had not attempted suicide the day after I finally told Hew about B.W....

Hew was in fact considering leaving me—but not in the way I suspected.

Anyway as I've said change doesn't happen so much as it accumulates. Dust and gas gather. Matter gloms and gloms, spinning. Not suddenly, but eventually, an explosion...

You would be forgiven for forgetting all about the anarchists. Certainly I did. But they'd had grand visions from the outset, starting with the Action in Philadelphia, having narrowly escaped the Knights of Right. Hew and the chefs and the anarchists had gone out on the scaffolding outside their friend's window and stayed up all night. Hew had lain back on the plywood floor, making an angel in the sawdust and ground plaster. Later he stood, massaging his battered hands, leaning out over the flashing, eerie street. Everyone smoked, talked, reflected. In Hew, probably in everyone who was paying more attention than I was, fury sprouted and grew.

One thing these fascists and religious fanatics get right, one of the anarchists said, is that the so-called culture war is a real fucking *war*. This is never going to end with kumbaya. One way of life or the other, ours or theirs, is going to be *extinguished* eventually. *They* know it's existential and it's about time we all woke up to that. All this smug liberal, live-and-let-live, coexist bullshit . . . we have got to stop *pretending* that we're fine with these dogmatic repressive religious hicks as long as they stay out of Brooklyn. They're living and voting and buying *guns* in *our* country. We need to totally marginalize and defeat these people, or at least reeducate their children.

One of the chefs said, We've had one civil war, you know? One half of the country literally *conquering* the other half. We could do it again.

Figuratively speaking, said Hew.

Sure, yeah, said the chef.

Or not figuratively, said an anarchist.

After this they talked about RIP for a while. In many ways RIP was even more bothersome than the Knights of Right because it was *permitted,* lawful. How could it be that no instrument of government or popular sentiment was capable of stopping B.W. Rubin? The place was a national disgrace, Hew said, and all agreed. The

Knights were dumb thugs; B.W. was Pablo Escobar. He was holding his country hostage, turning government inside out. Hew described life at RIP—the curriculum, the culturally appropriative teas on Wednesdays, the robot delivery carts, concierge medical care, heated bidet toilet seats, the perverse pristineness of it all—in terms that absolutely enraged these anarchists who lived ~2% above the poverty line.

The anarchists said, We should burn that place to the ground.

This seemed obviously hyperbolic until they explained about a cousin who worked in demolition who had been helping them stockpile C-4 for the right occasion.

The chefs were like Yeah, yeah, but they were at this point pretty high.

Hew said, You are out of your fucking minds, ha ha ha.

Police lights echoed and sirens squeezed down the narrow Philly streets and the anarchists said, See? A war zone. That big dick building, what's it called?

The Endowment.

Now *that* is a perfect target. The Death Star.

Hew had that teenage feeling of not knowing which side of irony everyone around him was on. It was like when his high school soccer team had gotten riled up on the idea of smearing dog shit under the floor mats of a rival team's goalie's Camry, and all Hew could think about was how that was actually the goalie's mom's car and if they did this *she* would have to pay a hundred bucks getting the car steam-cleaned. He still regretted saying nothing to put a stop to that, but he was grown now and when the anarchists refused to let the idea drop, he said: This is nuts. You're not killing anybody, and if you keep talking about this I'm going inside.

That put the issue on ice. They all tried to refocus on the *beauty* of the day, all those voices in Action together until they were violated by violence.

The conversation was not dead, however. These anarchists had found their calling. This C-4 was burning a hole in their pockets. Now they knew how to spend it. The Endowment was the best target they could think of by far. Unbeknownst to Hew they started planning. They kept in touch with Hew over Signal—a secure app, disappearing messages, end-to-end encrypted, etc.—but declined to mention that they were now studying how you take a building down, where you'd plant the charges, the most user-friendly detonators.

Hew had always made friends easily and thought that was what was happening: shared trauma generating a bond. The anarchists were very cool; they were clever; they were new friends. It did not occur to Hew until much later that he was being groomed, just as it probably did not occur to the anarchists that what they were doing might be called grooming. They thought they were just getting some information; maybe they were using Hew, yes, but only slightly, benignly. And to make sure *he* would not get hurt.

So there was a genuine mutual attraction in this relationship. Hew had an innate if essentially academic interest in American zealotry, fringe ideology. This traced, probably, to how totally Wonder Bread Hew's own upbringing had been. He was interested in how true radicals struggled with a nonradical system. He admired people who committed, who allowed the struggle to define them. These anarchists liked Hew because he was easy to like. And at the Institute he had an intriguingly foreign life. Hew's reports were like colonial dispatches from Darkest Africa.

More and more conversations crept up to the border of We really should *do* something about this place.

Ultimately the anarchists did not have to try that hard to build an argument, because the turn of events made its own case. After Philadelphia, there was that provocative footage of the Thanksgiving party, B.W. with scotch, above the demonstration in which Hew—and, unbeknownst to me, the anarchists—had chanted for hours. Then Melissa's assault, and Hew meeting Melissa. Then B.W. welcoming those kids from the Knights of Right forum, flaunting it in the *Wall Street Journal,* and *using the Endowment as a symbol of his vision for society!* As the Endowment engorged with symbolic meaning, so too, of course, did the possibility of its collapse, the power of rendering the Institute flaccid. Then came Perry's memorial service and the nonprosecution of Melissa's rape. Our fight; our endless fighting. Then finally Melissa's suicide attempt and my report of what B.W. had done to me...

But obviously obviously *obviously* you could *never* really do it. People would be killed or maimed. Out of the question.

Except what if there was a way to first evacuate the building?

Also, Hew wondered, was it possible the anarchists were

going to do what he now sensed they were planning, but *without* his involvement and *without* the scrupulous regard for human life that any plan would entail if he were part of it?

The police: a nonoption. It would have been the clear move except that Hew could never quite tell how serious the anarchists were being. Because the anarchists' messages were carefully phrased and disappeared after ten minutes, he had no real evidence of what they might or might not be contemplating. Plus he liked them. Plus he hated cops. Plus was he already a co-conspirator?

Hew did not exactly realize he was being swayed. Sometimes he could convince himself that this back-and-forth with the anarchists was no more than an inside joke, a bit they were all doing. When one day Hew stood on our dining table to read the exact model of the smoke detector, and when he thereafter confirmed that this was the kind of smoke detector that would also, when an alarm was pulled, start an infrared heat scan that fed into software that told firefighters and the sprinkler system exactly where the fire was and which rooms still had living creatures inside—and when he thought that yes this was the kind of system that could be used to ensure that no one was left inside a building before blowing it up—this was all a kind of fanciful thought experiment, like talking with the other IT guys over lunch about so if you were going to hack a government agency which one and why and how would you do it.

Perhaps the key indicator that Hew was always more serious about this idea than he was willing to admit to himself was that he did not say peep about it to me. We had talked a bit about the anarchists in the weeks after Philadelphia. Then they dropped completely from my radar of people in Hew's life. He did not even tell me that the anarchists he'd met in Philly had also come to the Thanksgiving protest, wanting to see the Endowment for themselves. Later Hew explained that he must have been worried about making me an accomplice. That maybe he was a little ashamed. Later he conceded that this rather significant secret of his might have contributed to the emotional distance between us.

As it turned out, Hew had never seriously considered leaving me. I had correctly identified that he was having dark, drastic thoughts—but they were mostly aimed elsewhere, not at me. I had underestimated Hew's patience for me. I suppose I was predisposed, for obvious Mom-related reasons, to fears of sudden abandonment. But Hew had always seen—or he later claimed he had always seen—that the incessant political conflict bubbling in our relationship was predominantly situational and that it would die down once we took it off the burner, i.e., left the Institute. He was very often frustrated with me but had intended, or so he said, to wait me out. I'm still not sure whether I believe him about this.

But unquestionably he had the finer social antennae of the two of us. He knew what I didn't, quite: that we were, that the whole Institute was, attempting to defy the laws of social and political physics. No situation this strange or volatile could last. One way or another we would come to ground, given time.

In the meantime, he needed distraction. Online. It was absence, yes, but also *so engaging*. The internet was like a climbing wall. It was stressful and required contorted human postures, and you learned as you did it. It was implicit in participation that the goal was to find higher and firmer footing. Hew loved finding the creative, strong, dexterous arguments that situated someone where others wished to be. He was an absolute sucker for this contest. One time while bickering about how phone-bound he was, I had called Hew a Web Supremacist, to which he said *mea culpa*.

So Hew was pretty miserable and exceptionally Online and he thought he had long been a socialist but no— now he was *really* discovering the blueprint for a more just society. Six months prior he would have said he supported universal basic income. Now he could tell you that UBI was crude and instead there was a way to use our ocean of data to identify the neediest people in real time and then to instantly send cash to their phones. Baseline equality looked blunt and unjust compared to the sophisticated system for rebalancing and redistributing wealth in real time that Hew envisioned. Society would not need to altogether abandon the idea of private property if it could instead make everyone's property a bit less private.

He drafted a gorgeous scheme in his head like a new Constitution. This idea was, it should be said, not totally implausible from a computing point of view. Machine learning was already good enough, in theory, to implement the mechanism Hew grew fixated on: a world of so-called dynamic equity, resting on an AI system smarter than any single person but built out of and thus completely human in its judgments, such that it would be immune to stock conservative criticisms re: the vast bureaucratic overhead and moral hazard concerns of a welfare state. The system would take and give in real time, completely transparently—so you could see, when you were taxed, who received the money and why the system thought they needed it, and vice versa you could see whose money you were receiving—and using blockchain, all of this could happen with trivial transaction costs, *sans* potential for Soviet-style corruption because the system itself had no mouths to feed, no interests but the collective. The system would reveal and reinforce the many ways people depended on one another; it would be the artificial intelligence that brought society together, made *society* into one collective intelligence. You could see your tax dollars at work; or on the other side of the equation you could appreciate what others were giving up on your behalf. Through constant feedback, dynamic equity would be honed and automated, improving itself, our incentives, and all of our lives until anything resembling class separation dissolved, and everyone could live with dignity and get precisely what they deserved, Hew thought.

The salient obstacle, he came to think, was vested interests. We *had* the technical capability; now it was time to find the political will. The search for and connection with other like-minded political fantasists became Hew's project. It was not Melissa but these fellow travelers (and the anarchists) with whom Hew had spent months in a relentless digital dialogue.

If I'd followed Hew Online I might have figured out what he was so into. But I had no stomach for his digital avatars. I had snooped, just once, for traces of Melissa. But finding nothing, I went back to avoiding his digital presence as thoroughly as we both now avoided meat; it was for our collective health.

And for his part Hew was not about to press dynamic equity as a topic of conversation. In retrospect I could remember him using that phrase, "dynamic equity," but I had never asked what he meant, and he wasn't going to try to initiate me if I was incurious. He could picture me hearing the AI redistribution idea and immediately identifying some unsolvable flaw in the mechanism, the bias that would be inextricable from the algorithm and that would only exacerbate over time. He was sure I would Yuck his Yum. It's true I probably would have. How, I would have asked him, do you ensure that the system is fed with the right data? Who decides what inputs it receives and who ensures no one is gaming it? Is it possible to appeal or correct a perceived misjudgment? Crucially, who defines the success metrics? How will the system accommodate and provide for outliers—like myself for instance—who have idiosyncratic preferences and/or the potential to bring so-far-unseen and thus so-far-unaccounted-for benefits to mankind?

By the time B.W. did what B.W. did to me—and by the time Melissa's attempt to drown herself was reported—Hew was probably ninety percent of the way to telling the anarchists, Okay, let's do it. He was already so furious all the time. And either the anarchists were persistent or the idea itself was persistent. It nagged. It had hung around long enough to normalize itself. Hew thought a lot about John Brown and Bill Ayers and the Boston Tea Party, the tradition of nobly lawless extremism that had, from time to time, started brush fires of revolutionary progressive thinking. Perhaps, Hew thought, he *could* fix one big thing? Perhaps, Hew thought, leveling the Endowment would accelerate the end of predatory capitalism and the beginning of dynamic equity in America? This seemed oddly, increasingly plausible.

For a while I'd been unable to tell him, or anyone, about B.W. I was determined to have better things to think about. I was determined to solve the problem on my own. I did feel like a victim, but not of B.W.—I felt like a victim of myself. I thought: *How* could you have failed to read *the contract*? This is America! The first rule is *always* read the contract, because *this* country will honor whatever it says. It was your own sloppiness, Helen, your own *impatience* with and *lack of rigor* regarding everything that is not physics that put you in this position. It was your own *stupid,* lifelong assumption that your talents make you immune to predation that let you walk into that situation blind, ill-equipped.

I do have a tendency toward self-blame. I'll defend it to the extent that I think people are better to err in that direction than the opposite. But at the heart of it was my need for control. I took responsibility even where I obviously wasn't responsible, because this illusion allowed me the secondary illusion that there was something I might have done, and might do next time, to change a bad outcome. Often I could not shake this intuition even when it was facially absurd. As a kid I was, for years, convinced that Mom would have survived if I had paid closer attention and promptly reported what I retrospectively decided were portentous signs of an impending embolism. It was just not plausible, I thought, that a fatal human malfunction would not provide *some* warning to the truly alert observer. To this day I remain sure on an emotional level that this is true. This despite the fact that the kind of pulmonary embolism that killed her has zero symptoms until it strikes.

One morning, though, I found myself saying, Hew, I have to tell you something. A few days had passed since I'd gone to B.W.'s penthouse. Or maybe a week. Time from this period is not crisp for me. I do remember Hew was putting his shirt on, this green gingham button-down I loved, and I stood in the bedroom doorway, wearing jeans and flats.

He looked up.

That night when I went up to B.W.'s—that wasn't nothing.

What do you mean?

He wanted me to sleep with him.

Hew stopped buttoning his shirt. Like, he touched you?

No, I said. It was—it was like he wouldn't let himself. He threatened me, and then he sat down next to me and then *leaned* very, very close. I put my right hand near my face, showing where B.W. had been.

He threatened you? Hew's mouth looked like it was melting off his face.

I nodded.

How did he threaten you?

Suddenly I could not quite talk. I realized I could not even gesture at the whole truth of the matter. There was too much to conceal, too much to regret. Of course I could not mention offering myself to Lens, which minutes after leaving Lens's house I could hardly believe I'd done. And I could not tell Hew about having solved HTS either: telling Hew would violate B.W.'s ironclad nondisclosure clause—and might, I worried, implicate Hew himself in the actions B.W. would bring against me. Plus what I'd done, what I'd discovered, still felt ludicrous, not believable. I had yet to say it aloud to anyone, even to myself. Saying it would be like announcing I'd had a brief, cordial meeting with God. Maybe this dissociative feeling, the seeming irrelevance of my own memories—both re lunging at Lens and solving HTS— was a by-product of trauma? In any case B.W. had my computer locked away, so I could not at the moment *demonstrate* that the model really worked, and it was against my training to assert anything scientific without evidence...

Hew didn't press me. Of course he knew better than to press me, or any woman, on such a subject. All Hew could see, in our misaligned state, was that I had been harmed and was extremely distressed. He thought I was cowed, inert.

Hew, however, was unusually uncowed, unusually ert. A cloud within him collapsed on itself, and next thing he knew he was on Signal. Hew, always supremely self-aware, so attuned to his own tropes, wondered even as he was doing it whether this was the scene where our hero is finally moved to action or whether this was the scene where a man, broken by circumstance, first gives in to his worst impulses and becomes our villain.

In any case the anarchists were ready. They had a plan.

44.

On the day they did it, winter was finally knuckling under. Small green buds grew like pustules on the cherry trees that dotted the Endowment lawn.

I had been walking the island a lot, avoiding everyone but store clerks and baristas. I had nothing else to do. I had no idea that Hew was up to anything. I was trying to solve the B.W. problem: how to get my model and myself out from under him. Actually that is misleading. I *wished* to solve the B.W. problem—I was *fixated* on the B.W. problem—but it's not right to say that I was really trying to solve it. I was not thinking scientifically, deliberately, logically. Instead I had been going into town and buying tchotchkes: a stone metate for grinding masa, which I had never done and had no intention to do, for instance. Also two silk scarves, two pairs of hand-carved chopsticks with wood stands, seven succulents, lavender perfume. Between boutiques I drank serial espresso, so that when I got home I would drop my bright shopping bags by the door and lie on the couch, stiff and vibrating.

Meanwhile Hew cracked the Endowment's fire alert system.

Meanwhile the anarchists rented a thirty-eight-foot Boston Whaler, loaded it with C-4, and docked it in the marina at Plymouth Island.

All of this, accomplished with essentially no obstacles. The fire alert system: barely, obsoletely encrypted. It took Hew ten minutes to find the hacking tool he needed, and just another six hours to use it. The anarchists found loading a rented boat with C-4 to be as straightforward as stocking a fishing trip. Later Hew remarked on how remarkably dangerous a person can be if he does not intend to get away with it, if he intends to be held accountable— or of course if he knows he won't be. There is not much, outside ourselves, to prevent any of us from doing our worst.

One day, midafternoon, a voice came from the smoke detectors in every room in the building: ATTENTION. ATTENTION. THE ENDOWMENT HAS BEEN RIGGED WITH EXPLOSIVES AND WILL BE DE-MOLISHED SHORTLY. PLEASE CALMLY PROCEED TO THE NEAREST FIRE EXIT AND REMOVE YOURSELF FROM THE VICINITY. THIS IS NOT A DRILL. THIS IS NOT A DRILL.

By the time the message looped, Hew was standing by the door with bags and jackets for both of us. The voice in the detectors was Hew's.

This is not a drill?

It's not, he said. Let's go.

Is it wrong that, as I followed Hew down the hall and into the stairwell, I really wanted to kiss him?

We entered the flow of confused but unpanicked people filtering down the stairwell, draining across the lawn. The conversations I overheard indicated that no one quite believed what Hew's voice in the smoke detectors had announced. Probably it was a badly conceived prank. Hew, in contrast, moved definitively. At some point he had taken my hand. He pulled us across campus and down the hill. I had some sense of where he was leading us.

Hew, I said. Was that warning literally true? The building is coming down?

Yes.

And you—

We're not going to kill anyone.

Are you sure?

I can explain when we get there.

At Perry's bungalow, Hew led us around to the back patio and then inside through the French doors, which were unlocked. Someone had tidied up. There were no dishes in the sink. When he was alive, Perry was predisposed to leave at least one dish uncleaned at all times; I now like to think this was a principled stab against sterility, a policy of accepting the inevitable sooty byproducts of human existence. Perry's belongings remained but the place was too spotless, his absence too apparent.

Hew opened his laptop on the dining room table and showed me the software that allowed him to track which parts of the building remained occupied. I studied the screen's reflection in his glasses. His honed, stubbled face wore a look of simple focus. Less than thirty minutes had elapsed since the first warning but the Endowment was already almost empty.

We watched red dots move toward exits and dwindle, and meanwhile Hew explained to me about the anarchists, about how they had come here on a Boston Whaler and had, over the course of yesterday, shuttled, on the Institute's autonomous carts, a large volume of explosives from the wharf up to the Endowment. Throughout the Endowment's deep basement, they had pinned charges to the central structural spine. On every floor of the building, this extravagantly engineered spine was a prominent design feature, and the demolitionist cousin had said that if they put enough explosives anywhere on that thing they could sever it, and then the whole building would topple.

The anarchists were presently about a mile offshore on the Boston Whaler, with remote detonators, awaiting Hew's confirmation that the Endowment was vacant.

This is totally insane, I said. I was not feeling overwhelmed—in fact I was very clear, quite calm—but it seemed necessary to acknowledge the cliché that some objective observer would be thinking. Moments of high drama cause me, like many people I think, to see myself cinematically.

Have you actually gone insane? You're going to go to prison for this.

Unquestionably, said Hew.

I kissed him.

I said, Don't blow the place yet. I have to go get
something.

What?

My laptop.

It's in your bag, isn't it?

I shook my head. My work laptop. Locked in the lab.
B.W. confiscated it because I solved HTS and he wants to
keep the model proprietary. That's . . . that's why I went up
there when—

Hew tried to determine whether I was joking, and
then, deciding I wasn't, laughed. *Now* you tell me?

Can you hold them off?

You *solved* it?

Yes, and let's not un-solve it by blowing the place up. It's
bad enough you're about to incinerate all our other stuff.
Can you hold them off?

They are militant anarchists, so who knows. But yes,
I think so.

I headed for the door.

Hew said, Uh, don't dawdle. Once the police and bomb
squad get here . . .

I'll run, I said.

I jogged along the winding campus paths, cut across
the green, passed puzzled people all heading in the other
direction, away, and finally arrived at the back of the
observing crowd. The crowd draped across the paths and
yards around the Endowment like a frayed mop end. I
jostled past a Pulitzer winner and his dogs, a Broadway
producer, the two inseparable Fields Medalists. People had
formed a perimeter around two hundred yards out. There

was no cordon or barrier, just a few security guards and an assumption that this distance *should* be safe enough? In the sky, a few drones and one news helicopter paced, circled, waiting.

I was alone crossing the lawn in that direction. Behind me a few people yelled Ma'am! Hey, lady! In the atrium two people in wheelchairs rolled themselves toward the door, their laps laden with backpacks and duffel bags.

Hew had activated the emergency lighting. The basement hallways were dim, interrupted by bursts from strobes on the ceiling. All around, the repeating sound of Hew's voice. My access card had gotten me into the stairwell and into the basement, but I remained locked out of the lab.

The only choice was to break in, so I went to the lounge and gathered a metal chair and a toaster oven, the two items I thought most likely to help me shatter the door's narrow, heavy glass pane. Nonetheless, I could not generate sufficient concentrated force. Barely a scratch.

Hew was now calling me.

A police helicopter is about to land on the island, he said. The others are freaking out at me for letting you go back inside.

While he talked, I stalked the halls looking for a sharp, dense object. Then, on the wall: duh. The bright red box. Break Glass in Emergency.

The axe, having no alternative, axed. I reached through the open panel, turned the handle. I was in.

But all my stuff was gone. Not just the laptop but the PC. Perry's too.

I called Hew back.

Did you get it? he said.

It's gone. B.W. took it away somewhere.

You've got to get out of there. You're the only one left, except B.W.

B.W. is still inside?

Well, someone is in his study.

Do the elevators work?

Helen...

I'm going up.

45.

Waiting for the elevator, I was surrounded by the Endowment's spine. In the crevices and acute angles sat gloms of plastic explosive, smudged there like schoolroom boogers. Embedded in the C-4, remote detonators the size of Hot Wheels.

That was a long elevator ride, heading up forty-seven floors. My ears popped. My hair tingled. My gut was lead.

The door opened on B.W.'s Roman statuary. Emergency strobes dyed the sculptures intermittently red on one side. Through the window at the corridor's end: drones, multiple helicopters, boats in the Sound, with more of each coming. They were here to see the fireworks. In some sense they must have been rooting for Hew, because if you really thought people were going to die you might not go out of your way to so brazenly spectate. Or maybe you would?

The penthouse door was unlocked. It was impossible, in

the great room, not to hope that some of these irreplace-able artworks and artifacts might survive. Hew had never been up here and did not know the treasures he would be immolating, but that was hardly Hew's concern. The museums were to blame, I thought; they had forfeited these items' rights to be preserved by selling them to B.W. Rubin. My model on the other hand: stolen. Technically not, I guess, as a matter of contract, but still stolen in my view. Certainly I had not ever consciously decided that my discovery ought to be B.W.'s property, or anyone's. So I had a right to reclaim it, to pluck it from the imminent wreckage.

Two police helicopters—a strange thing to see from above—floated onto the lawn steeply below me.

In the study: those bookcases, the leather couches, the vast desk, the Yale telescope. B.W. reclined on one of the couches, his impeccably loafered feet crossed on the coffee table. He was reading a stack of papers—probably, I thought, the proprietary competitive information of some business he intended to hostilely acquire. He looked up at me over his reading glasses. The *loathing* I felt...

I was not, I should say, remotely afraid of B.W. in this moment. I was more afraid of myself, of enacting one of the extravagant murders I'd been internally simulating.

Helen?

For the first time in our history, B.W. seemed genuinely surprised to see me.

I need my laptop. My model.

Oh, it's quite secure. Have you decided about my offer?

If I accept, will you give me the laptop? Now?

His smile: playful, villainous. He was enjoying himself. The model was backed up in the cloud, and I would have to persuade him to give me access later. For now, I saw, he was not going to budge. Two drones hovered immediately outside the study window, watching us. We were out of time.

You can't stay here, I said. This is not a prank. I have that on good authority.

Did *you* do this? Again I seemed to have surprised him.

I know who did. I've seen the explosives.

But it's not you.

No.

He looked relieved. He said, Well, *they* are not going to do anything. These people—he fluttered a hand dismissively toward the window, indicating the entire limp-dicked liberal world—these people lack the killer instinct. They have been waiting for everyone to evacuate. So I am not going to evacuate.

I . . . I don't think you're right about that, I said. I tried to say it slowly, with a sense of significance.

The arrogance, the *calm* of him. He said: I guess we'll find out.

On the way out, I stole the antique Japanese cricket cages.

I was not, on the way down, thinking about how if B.W. was killed I might never get my model back, about how it would be squirreled like the Ark of the Covenant in a billionaire's encrypted digital warehouse, forever inaccessible to me.

The police clutched me as I exited the Endowment. They didn't ask about the cricket cages. They wanted to know the situation inside. Had I seen what appeared to be explosive devices? Yes. Everywhere. With remote detonators. Had I been up in the penthouse—was I the last person out of that floor? They were wondering whether the red dot they could see—the same one Hew could see—was a person or a large animal or a glitch. I explained that B.W. remained in his study, that he was determined to stay. Several nearby windbreakers debated whether to risk sending in the bomb squad. After a couple of minutes they took my name and I was allowed to go.

By the time I got back to Perry's, B.W. had posted a video explaining, in that same sickening condescending calm tone he had just used with me, why he refused to leave his Endowment.

As I entered the house, Hew silently gestured for me to stay in the kitchen, out of sight of his laptop camera. He and the anarchists were arguing, and Hew was recording.

The gist of Hew's position was: He called our bluff. We *agreed* when I said I'd help you that we would *not* kill *any*one. Not one person. That's all there is to it. Maybe someone will get him out of there but until they do, you are not touching that button.

The gist of the anarchists' position was: *FUCK B.W. RUBIN!!* He thinks we don't have the *stones* to blow *him* up?? Who knows how long we have before the police figure out where we are? We're not waiting for someone to *coax* him out of his stupid fucking tower. We are doing it. Go ahead make my day motherfucker...

Hew said, NO.

46.

I will go to my grave still curious about what went through B.W.'s mind when he heard the first crack, the first rumble. There is drone footage of him at the moment it happened. He was as I'd left him: reclining on a sofa in his study, feet up, reading papers. The obvious question: Do people that rich *really* believe themselves to be immortal, favored and protected by the gods? He was the absolute perfect picture of superiority, of pride before fall.

Well, he did not exactly, only, fall. First he went *up*.

The anarchists' demolitionist cousin—accustomed to bringing down brittle 1960s concrete—had been able to do only so much coaching. Normally when you demolished a building you first did structural studies. What the cousin had offered were some rules of thumb and a reasonable guess about how to go about it.

No one had realized quite how unusually thick the metal of the Endowment's spine was, or how redundant and dense its structural lattice. It had been built with no expense spared and likely could have withstood a nuclear strike.

So the explosion, simulations showed, had first gone *out* from the spine, shredding the walls, floors, and servers in the Endowment basement. Immolating the 522-petaflop supercomputer. Incinerating my laptop and PC, my model, which records later revealed had been locked in a storage room two doors down from my lab, and I could have retrieved them if I'd known. Beyond this the explosion met the uncompromising rock of Plymouth Island.

There remained, however, a *great* deal of excess energy. The only outlet now was up. The Endowment's spine operated like the barrel of a gun. Or a urethra if you like. The explosion, contained within the central tube, tore up through floor after floor, sweeping all that concrete and steel and eight tumbling elevators up up up until it ended, capped by the Endowment's top floor.

Finally, there, release. A pillar of flame.

B.W.'s comeuppance. He and his entire penthouse, ejaculated five hundred feet skyward.

The crowd below scrambled away, and this is where most reported injuries came from: turned ankles, broken hands and noses. The debris landed mostly in the woods and water. One mangled elevator plummeted through the roof of a Pulitzer winner's greenhouse. B.W.'s remains were never identified.

At the first subterranean rumble, Hew and I ran outside to see. For a while we stood on Perry's patio and watched the Endowment burn like the Olympic torch. Hew was behind me, his arms draped around my waist, his chin beside my right ear. I listened to him breathing. I loved him so fucking much in that moment. Can I say, without sexism, that I knew he was my *man* again?

It took me years to sort out why this moment opened so much up for us: probably I'm still sorting it out. To be clear, the thing I felt for Hew just then was not about violence or vengeance, exactly. It was not about him being dangerous or unmeasured. The thing, I think, was that Hew exploding the Endowment was so *personal*. He had felt *compelled*. He could not have known how the world would receive it. Yet his whole future and my future and every object he owned—every object *I* owned—were placed squarely on the line. As we watched the Endowment spew fire, I sensed a peace within him; his long limbs were at ease. I felt the contented embrace of someone who had tried to do what he felt he must.

After the initial flames, a plume of smoke drifted, at times flimsy and Vatican-like, from the circumcised tip of the structure. The rest of the building glowed, especially after dusk fell. What little material remained inside the Endowment's spine smoldered and burned. The lovely faint orange light of a dying star emanated through the building's exterior.

All right, Hew said, it's time for me to go. He placed his laptop in his satchel as casually as if he were heading to a café for the afternoon.

You're turning yourself in?

I had asked but already I knew. If we had spent months misaligned, disharmonious, the explosion had jolted us back into place. It was the missing chip; my sensors worked again. I could intuit his thoughts and flow with them the way I sometimes flowed through programming. Hew did not think he was righteously above society. He had done this *for* people, *for* society, so now he had to submit to law and public judgment, to a jury of regular human peers— the way men like B.W. never voluntarily would.

I said, I'll come with you.

47.

Police helicopters and cruisers littered the Endowment lawn. The air fluttered with a snow of ash and dust. A limp cord of windblown police tape embraced the building's base. All of the lobby's windows had blown out; its furniture had toppled; art had cartwheeled off the walls. But the overall damage was slight except inside the spine, the glowing core. Uniformed men milled around because there was, basically, nothing to do at the moment. Fire and Rescue had determined to let the fire burn itself out, which it would likely do by morning.

Hew kissed me, and then we approached the nearest officer.

I'm here to turn myself in, Hew said. I was involved in planning what happened today. The evidence is on the laptop in this bag.

He opened the bag to show the bewildered officer that inside was only a MacBook, not another bomb. Then he handed the backpack over, knelt, and placed his long arms and big hands in the air. All done in perfect Hew fashion: deliberate, careful.

At this point Hew was savagely tackled. Soon he was facedown in the grass in cuffs, and I'd been grabbed and restrained, and for a while there was a lot of shouting.

Among the shouts was one officer saying into a radio that they had arrested two people who said they planned it.

Hew said, No, no! She didn't know anything about it! She wasn't involved. She's here because she's my wife!

You're his wife?

I said: Yes... I am. I emphasized the period at the end of the sentence. Hew and I were looking right at each other.

But I suppose it looked rather sinister to the police when two presumptive bombers began laughing and grinning at each other.

I was arrested along with Hew and the police interviewed me, on and off, until about 3 p.m. the following day, when I was released without charge into the streets of New Haven.

The Yale campus was littered with Solo cups and shattered bottles: the remnants of students celebrating, deep into the night, the demise of the Endowment and B.W. Rubin. To these people Hew wasn't bin Laden; Hew was the guy who'd killed him.

48.

The basic mechanism of superconductivity requires a phenomenon called Cooper pairing. This is where two electrons, which ordinarily repel each other due to their negative charge, become linked. It is a quantum effect but basically what happens is that the vibrations in a positively charged atomic lattice overpower the natural mutual repulsion of electrons and press them into a bond. The pairing is delicate, easily broken by thermal energy (i.e., heat). This is why Cooper pairing, and so superconductivity, is rare except at very low temperatures. Other conditions must obtain too.

Cooper pairing enables superconductivity because the two electrons, paired together, are less prone to so-called scattering events—the little jostles and interruptions to forward movement that single electrons experience when buffeted by various other forces. When paired, electrons are stronger, harder to disturb. They resist resistance. Together electrons can move resiliently through obstacles that would divert either of them alone. These paired electrons' efficient movement through the atomic lattice is the prized effect: superconductivity.

Like I said, many physics metaphors are overdetermined. It is rote at this point for condensed-matter physicists to refer to Cooper pairing as a lot like marriage.

Anyway I am fond of this particular metaphor.

The Institute never returned to its former—let's not say glory. For more than a year the Endowment was a towering husk, dark and hollow, while Institute trustees debated and insurers processed claims. With the Endowment uninhabitable, and with the rest of the island lacking sufficient accommodations or facilities, the displaced peoples of RIP occupied the hotels and motels of New Haven. The school became a distributed system. An additional ferry was leased to handle the extra traffic. The school hobbled forward.

The Endowment was eventually rehabilitated, and the Institute reassembled there, but it lacked the same offensive virility. The Institute had been, the joke was, vasectomized. The school's mission remained nominally the same. But where B.W. had once been the only governance, now a board of trustees had actual power to run the place. The board did what it is in the nature of committees to do: generated new committees and delegated to them. What had been B.W.'s towering palace apartment became a modest president's office within a humming hive of bureaucrats. Soon the top five floors of the Endowment were all administration and HR. It could have been any college anywhere.

The prosecutors threw the book at Hew, but most of

it missed. They leveled remarkably heavy charges given that Hew had told the police exactly where to find the anarchists—who had fled and were not as keen as Hew to be subject to a jury of purported peers—and given that Hew was the prosecutors' star cooperating witness. In the end he served seventeen months.

Hew's trial introduced the world at large to the concept of jury nullification. This is when, I learned, a jury recognizes that the accused person has done all of the things that constitute a crime but believes, for whatever reason, that the accused does not deserve the punishment for that crime, and so declines to convict despite the evidence. When this occurs the prosecutors are up a creek; there can be no retrial.

Hew's prosecutors had charged first-degree murder; they had tried for reckless endangerment; they had stacked federal conspiracy charges—explosives crossing state lines, etc.—such that the mandatory minimum sentence, if the jury had convicted on these counts, would have put Hew away for seventy-three years.

The jurors from Hew's case, interviewed later, all said the prosecutors had proven the facts—of course they had. But the case was not right. It was a lot more wrong, the jury thought, than what Hew had done. The punishment was not remotely proportionate. The jury had seen—the whole world had seen—the footage of Hew pleading with the anarchists not to blow the Endowment with B.W. still inside. They knew he had not wanted to kill anyone, that Hew had *insisted* on precautions. Hew had testified on his own behalf, against the advice of his lawyer, and by the end he had actually, very improbably, gotten the jury on his side. The assistant US attorney did not know what hit him. The law was against Hew but the pulse of the nation was with him, and he knew it. I watched him on the stand, so tall, so upright, so reasonable, so handsome. The jury declined to convict on every count besides first-degree criminal mischief.

The memoir that Hew wrote in prison became quite popular. People bought it for the intrigue and conspiracy, the crime and the subsequent legal drama. But Hew smuggled in his millennial vision of dynamic equity, and soon this idea had gone from Online niche to the *New York Times* op-ed pages. Pretty soon even *The Economist* ran an article titled: "It Is Time to Talk Seriously About Dynamic Equity." Immediately after his release, Hew was in demand as a speaker at conferences and colleges. As Hew became prominent, at least in policy circles, I hate to say it but I kept waiting for that thing you wait for with any famous man these days—for someone to come forward with an awful story about Hew, probably of the sex-monster variety. I've awaited the Cancellation of the Man Who Canceled Cancel U. But it hasn't arrived (yet).

Hew's finger was on the pulse. Dynamic equity was an idea whose time had come. It was radical but at the same time scratched a profound technocratic itch among the educated classes. It gave economists and computer scientists and policy wonks something to converse about, to convene over. Saying you were open to this system became stylish, the right opinion. In the tech world, it was the *only* opinion. For programmers, engineers, investors, billionaires who had made their fortunes collecting data for advertising—to imagine that their data and behavioral analytics could automate altruism and perhaps solve, in perpetuity, economic inequity in America—it made their deepest self-justifications plausible. These people had always insisted that their highly remunerated work would somehow also change the world for the better, and to prove themselves right several of the wealthiest men on the planet stood up an Institute for Dynamic Equity in Oakland.

Hew became a senior director of this new Institute. We sat on the dais at the ribbon-cutting, Hew as esteemed an intellectual as all the professors from Stanford. On the desk in his office at IDE, Hew kept two beautiful antique Japanese cricket cages. A gift from his spouse, he said, whenever anyone commented.

We were in one of our best phases, then, though Hew's prominence took some getting used to. It was hard to know what to make of the fact that his Online addiction—which I had always dismissed as at best a diversion if not genuinely deleterious to the critical faculties—had turned out to be such a fruitful investment of time. Out there in the great Online, Hew had honed his ear, his ability to decode the national dialogue, and in the process had learned to be influential in same. We were both finally figuring out that Hew was not an IT guy, and not a terrorist either; basically he was a politician. Not the kind who runs for office, but the kind who consults and advises, the kind who finds the right spin, who knows how to socialize a new idea with the chattering classes.

For a lot of people, myself included, this work would have been awful. But Hew was a pig in shit. It worked for him and so it worked for me. It was a lot easier to be happy myself when he was.

For years Hew and I debated what had happened to me, politically, during that year at the Institute. Hew liked to tease me about what he called my Libertarian Interregnum. But what I actually had, I posited, were Schrödinger's politics—a complement to Schrödinger's marriage and Schrödinger's affair. When I wasn't looking, I barely had politics at all—I had always been this way. When I did have to look, when I had to identify my position, my politics depended on the precise question presented and the point of observation. This is different from apathy, I think. There is strong science supporting the idea that I am not the only human being who is reactive and irrational in this way; that I am not alone in having moral intuitions that are little more than, well, intuitions—and one would never *expect* intuitions to be immune to circumstance or to hold the logic of a cohesive system.

One day Hew and I had lunch at his office. It was one of those days in Oakland's endless autumn, when the air is bright and thin and the sun toasts and shadows chill. I had come over, a half-expected surprise, with lentils from an Indian place we liked. Hew was in his office chair, tilted all the way back, his arms behind his head, his feet up on the big pouf he kept below his desk, his glasses low on his nose. For a moment I gazed at him through his office's glass wall.

Oh, wife, he said when I knocked. Are we having lunch?

We're having a meeting. I have an important idea we must discuss.

All right, he said. He clicked around for a moment, then swiveled his monitor to show me his calendar, on which he had marked the next hour with an appointment titled Helen's Important Idea.

Please, sit, he said.

I sat and proceeded to argue that people make political *commitments* as a kind of promise to *themselves,* and we do this precisely because our beliefs are not coin collections, are not persistently observable phenomena.

What do you think about that? I said.

Hew chewed pilaf and conceded that we mortals are, indeed, often uncertain about our true interior selves.

Therefore, I said, I think many of us *commit* to ideas and goals to avoid the impossible task of looking inward to *de novo* assess and reassess, moment by moment, in perpetuity, everything we believe. At some level, to function in real life, to avoid paralyzing self-consciousness, we must just decide what our values are and put doubts to bed.

But, I said, this process of *committing* to a belief contradicts the rational and scientific process—which tells us to adjust to new data, to change our minds when the evidence changes, and never to declare certainty beyond the well-proven. So you can see, right?, why *I* have always had difficulty with your desired level of political commitment? This idea of deciding to believe something—much less of committing to an entire complex political program inevitably premised on something as vague and mushy as moral intuition—is *inherently* anti-intellectual! Even if, I admit it, such commitments may be a best practice for personal happiness and responsible citizenship.

Well, yes, dear, Hew said. He was grinning.

What? I said.

You're cute.

I thought I had reached a deep insight but apparently it was all very obvious. Hew stood and went to his shelves. He pulled down three books and gave them to me. Apparently this conflict between intellectualism and activism was well-known, a persistent and oft-discussed tension in the academy.

Oh, I said. I thought I might be the first person to have thought of this.

Not this time. And anyway, even you can commit without proof. I've seen it.

When? I said. To what?

To me, he said.

I flicked a lentil that bounced perfectly off his smirking forehead.

49.

The HTS model I'd created back at RIP: alas, never recovered. A few months after the explosion, it became possible to make an appointment to collect your belongings. They had installed two construction elevators inside the hollow charred core of the Endowment. You put on a hard hat and rode up with your empty suitcases and boxes, packed your things—our apartment was undisturbed except for toppled vases and picture frames—and then the construction guys would help you load out. This was the last time Hew and I saw the Institute: riding away on the ferry, sitting atop our luggage like refugees from the Continent headed for Ellis Island.

Anyway while we were there collecting our things I was told, definitively, that nothing from the basement floor where my lab was had survived. I said: Truly zero? Not even a hard drive?

Zilch. It's dust and ash down there.

So I had to re-create what I'd lost. My key insight into

HTS was not the sort of thing I could forget. And one nice thing about the scientific method is that we work with an eye toward replicability. If others cannot redo what you've done, you haven't proved anything. So it was possible for me to retrace my steps, roughly.

I still fantasize about the original version of that model. I have never approached the elegance, the efficiency, of what I created in those mad final weeks at the Institute. Surely I am idealizing it, putting my lost work on a pedestal, but in the end it took me over three distracted months to re-create a functional version of my all-purpose HTS simulator, and the final version was still clunky. Version 2.0 took four days to simulate what Version 1.0 could have done in six hours.

That the model did the job was about the best that could be said of it.

And, well, doing this particular job was not nothing.

It seemed B.W. never told anyone about what I had done or about the intellectual property which his estate now technically owned. I guess when you attempt something especially evil, you keep it to yourself. In any case, if he did tell someone, no one followed up on the proposition B.W. had made to me.

So when I returned to Cornell, I felt free of claims and encumbrances. People had so much sympathy for me, this bright young woman whose world kept crumbling around her, that it was easy to secure a low-stipend fellowship. I let them think they were doing me a favor rather than the other way around. Cornell didn't know it was about to be the university that solved HTS.

Hew had gotten his revenge on B.W. Rubin. This was mine. The Institute would not get the credit for the greatest physics breakthrough in two decades. I was not going to be RIP's trophy, one of the great minds who had done her great work in those hallowed halls. Indeed what I said in interviews was that I'd had to *leave* the Institute in order to sufficiently focus on the problem. I wanted my success to invalidate the place.

The rest is nerd history. *Nature* published my paper to great excitement, and three years later I was summoned by the King of Sweden.

But surely you will have noticed that our world continues to trundle toward environmental catastrophe, that we do not presently have a lossless power grid, safe nuclear fusion, mass ocean desalination, personal supercomputers, home MRIs. HTS was solved—but HTS was not the answer. My model, and the many copies and variations of it that others constructed, made it simple to accurately simulate the superconducting potential of any atomic structure, any material, real or hypothetical. In the year after I published my first paper, hard condensed-matter physics around the world entered a frenzy of these simulations. The idea was to be the first to find the material that really worked at room temperature and near-sea-level pressure. But nothing did. Eventually you could see the trend line—an asymptote, a limit point, a boundary. The line incrementally approached but never crossed 147,000 atmospheres. Any lower pressure required far lower temperatures before superconductivity occurred.

What this meant was that there was no way to

manufacture the material we were all looking for; it could not exist.

Of course you could try to lower the cost of cooling or pressurizing. But this was an engineering problem, outside the theoretician's ambit.

Needless to say, the entire HTS world, myself included, was pretty deflated for a while. Nonetheless, the HTS limit point did produce additional questions. Why a limit point? Why *this* limit point? How did this quantum phenomenon produce what appeared to be a classical if strange thermo-dynamic trend line? So there remained plenty of work for me to do. In the end the major impact of my discovery was to finally end the HTS gold rush. It saved humanity some time and pushed physics, begrudgingly, on to the next task, the next potential frontier.

In my Nobel speech—and by this time it had become clear that HTS was not the panacea we had spent forty years pursuing—I spoke about Perry and the Wood-stock of Physics and the Institute and Hew, my infamous husband, who at that time remained two months from his release from prison. The trite point I tried to make was that even we, the physicists, a relatively rational and evidence-driven bunch, had succumbed to utopian think-ing. And as usual it had not panned out. But without these grand delusions, would we have learned what we eventu-ally learned? Would we have doggedly pursued HTS for four decades until it cracked? Would we keep pushing for those tiny increments of new knowledge; would we get any closer to the true asymptote, the limit point, of human understanding, ability, and justice? Winning a Nobel Prize was straightforward, I said. All you have to do is be optimistic without being wishful, be rigorous without losing creativity, be focused without being myopic. You just have to be certain but never too certain, determined but never too determined. Simple!, I said, and got a laugh.

A few weeks after I returned from Sweden, Leo Lens called. We had not talked in years, since my proposition—I'd been too mortified to face him. But then one day I became one of those people whom he called unsolicited in the late afternoons. He still lived at the Institute, and I could picture him pacing around his plain living room in an ancient cardigan, corduroys, and a telemarketer's headset. He always wanted to talk, first, about something very specific—usually some science thing he'd read—and after this was done, about anything at all.

When I picked up the phone the first time, his deep sandy voice said: Hi, it's Leo. I just watched your speech. *Blech*. So grandiose. Why didn't you let me write something for you? I've been writing Nobel speeches in my head for decades.

At any given moment, a lot about the world was changing, but never quite what you thought. You couldn't model where culture was headed—I mean, even *I* couldn't. So to Lens I said, Oh, you'll get your turn.

I'm pretty sure I believed that.

ACKNOWLEDGMENTS

More people than I can hope to name made a difference on the long path to this first novel. I'll try to thank you all individually.

My special thanks go to: Edward Parker, without whom Helen would not have known any physics; Noah Rosenblum and Ashwini Sukthankar, who got the manuscript into the right hands; Anna Tomlinson, Nick Hurwitz, and Jonathan Lethem, for astonishing generosity and insightful readings spanning more than a decade; and Vicki, Richard, Nora, Ella, Allison, and Sheep, for being my family.

On the professional side, my greatest thanks go to Emma Parry, a brilliant reader and advocate in a truly weird business, and to Jean Garnett, an editor of fearless taste and vision. Thanks also to the marvelous team that made the book real: Ali Lake, Paul Bogaards, Kate Downen, Khadijah Mitchell, Lucy Kim, Katherine Myers, Sabrina Callahan, Mariah Dwyer, Anna Brill, Linda Arends, Liv Ryan, and Barbara Perris.

ABOUT THE AUTHOR

Julius Taranto's writing has appeared in the *Washington Post, Los Angeles Review of Books, Chronicle of Higher Education,* and *Phoebe.* He attended Yale Law School and Pomona College. He lives in New York.